Mistletoe Mantra

"A
nea
her

Before she could even blink, he pressed his lips to hers. The kiss was firm and coaxing to begin with, but an unseen match lit her body on fire. Nomi's lips parted on a surprise gasp and Linc took advantage. His tongue dipped in and coaxed hers into a dance as it slid over.

White Hot Holiday

"Kiss me like I'm the only one that you want." She rolled her hips and did some type of two-step.

She was definitely the one he wanted, which of course was why he was here. For years, he'd been comparing his past girlfriends to Sage, which was crazy since he'd never actually dated Sage.

They weren't Romeo and Juliet, but there were definitely a few people from their families who had apparently picked up on their flirtatious ways in the past and hinted that he should stay away from Sage. Even his own sister had told him, *Once a playboy, always a playboy.*

Nana Malone is a *USA TODAY* bestselling author. Her love of all things romance and adventure started with a tattered romantic suspense she borrowed from her cousin on a sultry summer afternoon in Ghana at a precocious thirteen. She's been in love with kick-butt heroines ever since. You'll find Nana working hard on additional books for her series. And if she's not working or hiding in the closet reading, she's acting out scenes for her husband, daughter and puppy in sunny San Diego.

Books by Nana Malone

Harlequin Kimani Romance

Wrapped in Red with Sherelle Green

Visit the Author Profile page at
Harlequin.com for more titles.

Sherelle Green is a Chicago native with a dynamic imagination and a passion for reading and writing. Her love for romance developed in high school after stumbling across a hot and steamy Harlequin novel. She instantly became an avid romance reader and decided to pursue an education in English and journalism. A true romantic, she believes in predestined romances, love at first sight and fairy-tale endings.

Books by Sherelle Green

Harlequin Kimani Romance

A Tempting Proposal
If Only for Tonight
Red Velvet Kisses
Beautiful Surrender
Enticing Winter
Wrapped in Red with Nana Malone

Visit the Author Profile page at
Harlequin.com for more titles.

USA TODAY Bestselling Author

NANA MALONE
SHERELLE GREEN

Wrapped in Red

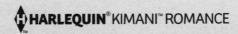

HARLEQUIN® KIMANI™ ROMANCE

ISBN-13: 978-0-373-86425-6

Wrapped in Red
Copyright © 2015 by Harlequin Books S.A.

The publisher acknowledges the copyright holders of the individual works as follows:

Mistletoe Mantra
Copyright © 2015 by Nana Malone

White Hot Holiday
Copyright © 2015 by Sherelle Green

PLEASE RECYCLE
THIS PRODUCT IS RECYCLABLE

Recycling programs
for this product may
not exist in your area.

For questions and comments about the quality of this book please contact us at CustomerService@Harlequin.com.

Printed in U.S.A.

CONTENTS

For everyone who has never ever had the courage to say I love you.

Dear Reader,

Lincoln Porter has loved Nomi Adams since they were kids. Now that she's finally coming home again, he has a chance to do something about it. I'm so thrilled to bring you Nomi and Linc's story. Theirs is about finding your way home and finding the courage to stand up and take what you want. They're spirited and fun and Linc is romantic enough to make any girl swoon. For a few years growing up I lived in a place just like Faith, Virginia, and I was more than happy to take the trip down memory lane with these two fun characters.

Romance the Sass,

Nana

If you don't want to miss a single Nana Malone romance, make sure you join my newsletter here: eepurl.com/blicGL

MISTLETOE MANTRA

Nana Malone

Chapter 1

"What do you mean, he said no?" Naomi "Nomi" Adams stared at her assistant, Ella Thompson.

Ella shook her head. "I'm sorry. I've tried everything. His agent, Ron. His Facebook. Hell, I even hired someone and *they* can't find him. The guy is a ghost. The only thing I've been able to dig up is that he lives in some place called Faith, Virginia."

Nomi's heart stuttered. *Oh hell*.

Belinda Foster, her managing editor, sat forward. "Didn't you grow up in Faith, Virginia, Nomi?"

Nomi swallowed hard and locked her jaw. Just thinking about her hometown was enough to make her ill. "Yeah, but I haven't been back in a long time."

Belinda sat back. "What do you suggest we do? This twentieth-anniversary special edition is supposed to be epic. You turned us on to this guy and he's perfect for the theme of beauty around the world. We have to find this guy."

The whole table looked at her for guidance. Four years ago Nolan Polk had burst onto the photography scene and become a media darling with an anti-bullying campaign he'd done with *Rolling Stone* magazine. They'd done a photo call, looking for up-and-coming photographers. After that he'd been extremely prolific. Everyone had wanted him. And then two years ago, he'd mysteriously stopped producing, only donating the occasional photograph for charity. It made him a hot commodity.

Unfortunately, he was also notoriously reclusive. *Sassy* magazine had been angling to get him to do a spread since he popped onto the scene. A photo from him would be the perfect addition to their twentieth-anniversary lineup. Though, that was only *if* they could get him. And that meant finding him first.

Nomi twirled her pen and tried to steer the direction of the conversation. "We don't have much time. If his rep won't get back to us, then we either need to find another photographer or get someone down there. I might know someone who can look into it for us."

Ella shifted in her chair. "I mean, I've tried everything. I even had our people in New York go down to his agent's apartment. No luck. Maybe his representation is out of town."

Or maybe Nolan Polk didn't *want* to be found. But it wasn't in Nomi's nature to back down from a challenge. Okay, not exactly true. She'd once run away from home and hadn't looked back on what she'd left behind, ever. But she was a whole new person now. The kind of person who got things done. "I'll get someone to Faith."

Belinda shook her head. "I think for something this

important, you need to go yourself. I mean, you are from there, after all."

Wait, what? No way, no how. "I'm sorry, what was that?"

Belinda pursed her lips as she always did when she was about to school someone. "You're from there. You know the locals. How hard will it be to ferret out one guy? You can do that in your sleep."

Nomi's skin went cold. She could do this. *No. No you can't. You can't go home to Faith.* "Well, I mean, it's the holiday and everything so I'm thinking there is a good chance even if I can track down where he lives, he won't be there." Not to mention that Faith was one of those towns that exploded Christmas holidays. And she, well, she hated everything about Christmas.

"Nomi, this is what we need right now. Can you commit to getting the job done?" Belinda asked.

Amber Divine leaned forward, perfectly curled red hair bouncing. "I can go if Nomi doesn't want to. I'm more than happy to be a team player."

Nomi gnashed her teeth together. She and Amber had been in the running for a senior editor position for months. If she let Amber go back to Faith and her competition got the Nolan Polk picture, there would go Nomi's promotion.

Her boss tapped her pen against her lips. "Actually, that's not a bad idea. Having more boots hit the ground will help."

Ella leaned forward. "We still have a week until Christmas. I can have you guys on the first plane out in the morning and scheduled to come back before the holiday. I know how you feel about Christmas—you'll be in and out."

"I really think it would be better to hire someone. Like a professional. Amber doesn't know the area and we'd be looking for a needle in a haystack," Nomi squeaked. She hated the idea of Amber doing what she couldn't.

Belinda frowned. "Why do I get the impression you don't want to do this?"

Because I don't. "Of course I do. I'm just worried we won't find him there during the holiday."

"Then let's hope you find a lead quick, because you're both heading to Faith."

Nomi slumped in her chair. If she was going home, then she'd need some reinforcements. And she'd have to make some arrangements. Ella was good at her job, but she didn't know Faith. They embraced the Christmas holiday like no place she'd ever seen. If there wasn't snow, they brought in snow machines to make sure it was a white Christmas. Every year, without fail. Tourists started pouring into the town right after Thanksgiving and didn't let up till the New Year. It made hotels and car rentals a nightmare.

As soon as the meeting was over, she trudged to her office and made a phone call she never thought she'd be making. At the same time she started an online search for a rental car and hotel. The Resplendence Inn seemed to have rooms, so she sent the link to Ella to book.

After three rings, a harried Jilly Porter answered the phone. "This is Jilly."

Nomi exhaled slowly. There was something comforting about her best friend's voice. "Hey, girl, it's Nomi."

"Nomi! Honey, it's been two months since we talked. Why is that? I wish I could chat, but I'm getting stuff ready for a shipment."

"Oh, sorry to catch you at a bad time. Real quick though, I'm coming home. Do you think you could swing a pickup from the train station tomorrow evening?" Faith was so small it didn't even have an airport, so she'd have to fly into Dulles, then take the train from there. *Planes, trains and automobiles.*

If possible, Jilly's voice went up an octave. "Home? Why? Holy shit, for how long? Are you going to see Brad? Are you going to tell your parents you're coming? Oh my God, of course you would call with news like this when I can't properly discuss."

Nomi couldn't help but smile. Jilly owned her own art gallery, and she also did private buying for select clients. "Short answers: yes, home, for work, hopefully no more than two days, hell to the no, and haven't decided yet. Now, can you pick me up from the train station or what?"

Jilly mumbled something and Nomi could only guess she was using her mouth to hold something while she did something with her hands. "I don't think I can do tomorrow night, but you know what? Linc probably can. He's here. You work out the deets with him and I'll see you as soon as you get in."

"Jilly, wait—" Nomi sighed. Jilly was notorious for delegating tasks without asking. Especially to her twin brother, Linc.

"This is Linc."

Nomi's brain stuttered; the voice she remembered wasn't the one on the line now. When had his voice gotten so deep? From the time she moved to Faith, she and Jilly had been inseparable. Which meant that everywhere they went, Linc hadn't been far behind. He and Jilly ran in the same circles at school, but Nomi could never say she knew him that well. He'd always been so quiet. More watchful than anything. He'd never needed to be the center of attention. And he'd helped get them out of more than a few scrapes thanks to her big mouth and Jilly's impulsive nature.

"Uh, Linc, hi. It's Nomi. Nomi Adams, from Faith."

There was a beat of silence. Then another beat. When he spoke again, his voice was low and raspy. "You honestly think I'd forgotten you? Without you, Jilly probably would have ended up as a rock star groupie or worse."

He had no idea how close he was with his teasing guess. She and Jilly had once snuck out to go to a Foo Fighters concert and Jilly had been hell bent on getting backstage by any means necessary, including flashing the bouncers her boobs if she had to. Nomi had managed to talk her out of it.

"Listen, I'm sorry to impose, but Jilly volunteered you to pick me up at the train station tomorrow night. I know it's a huge inconvenience, but I can't seem to get a single rental car in the area."

"Yeah, the holiday rush is in full swing." His voice was warm and mellow, like melting chocolate. "Not to worry. It's cool. Just text Jilly the details and I'll be there."

Good ol' Linc. "Thank you. It's much appreciated. I'll owe you one."

"I'll hold you to it." There was a beat of silence, then he said, "Last time I saw you, you said you were never coming back to Faith, Virginia."

Yeah, she had said that. And she'd meant it. "Apparently, never say never. I need to come back for work."

"You work for a magazine now, right?"

Nomi had no idea why, but just talking to him made her a little nervous, her skin heating. It must be the voice. It made it easy to forget she was talking to Jilly's brother.

"Yeah. They're sending me back to find Nolan Polk. He's supposed to live in Faith."

There was a long beat of silence. "What do you need him for?"

"Well, it's our twentieth-anniversary edition and we're looking for some of his photos for a spread."

"I don't get it. Wouldn't you normally call his agent or something? I assume a guy like that has an agent."

"Yeah, tried that. No luck. He isn't responding to our requests. So anyway, it appears I'm headed home to try and find him."

Linc's voice was soft, quiet. "Well, if anyone can find him, it's probably you. You always had a way of coming out on top."

Nomi swallowed hard as her brain conjured up an image of her on top of Linc, back arched in bliss. What the hell was wrong with her? Just because his voice was all grown and sexy didn't mean he'd grown with it.

"I hope you're right, Linc. I've got a lot riding on this."

Chapter 2

Nomi Adams was coming home. When Lincoln Porter hung up, he leaned his head back against the wall and shut his eyes tight. Caught somewhere between elation and dread, his brain tried to make sense of what she'd said. He'd had a thing for Nomi since she'd moved to Faith, but she'd never noticed him. She'd always treated him like a brother.

"You should look happier. *Why* don't you look happier?"

Linc peeled an eye open to glare at his twin sister. She matched him in coloring, from her inky black hair to her jade green eyes. Her features were softer, more feminine versions of his, down to the slight dimple in her chin. The only dissimilarity was the foot difference in height. She liked to tease that he'd stolen all her height genes. "That was low, Jilly. You should have given me some warning."

"Now, why would I want to do that? Besides, are you going to pretend that you don't *want* to see Nomi?"

"I don't know what you're talking about." He handed her back her phone. At times like this, he regretted the two of them being so close. It was impossible to hide anything from her.

"Bull. Five years is a long time to hold a torch for someone, little brother."

"Only by a minute, Jilly."

She slid him a sideways glance. "What? You thought you were slick back then? Come on, for the most part you were pretty shy, but the moment Nomi was around, you had to peek out of your little shell and hang around."

Linc pinned a narrow-eyed gaze on his sister. Lucky for him, he'd outgrown that shy awkwardness and he'd filled out. No one would call him awkward and skinny now. But five years was a long time. The last time he'd seen Nomi, she'd been running for the first train out of town after her dumb-ass boyfriend had chosen Lila Banks, or rather the Banks money and connections, over Nomi.

"Did you tell her?"

His sister's brow furrowed. "What? No! I was hoping you would get the balls and do it yourself. But I guess you never did."

The night she'd run away, Nomi had turned up at his house looking for Jilly to give her a ride. But his sister hadn't been there. Nomi had walked the two miles over from the country club in the rain after Brad had dumped her, and she had been soaked through.

When she'd asked him to swing by her house so she could grab her stuff and then take her to the train station, he hadn't tried to talk her out of it. Maybe because it hadn't hit him till they were on the platform that she was actually leaving. His stomach still knotted whenever he remembered what he'd said to her then. "You always deserved better than him."

Her smile had been sad, wistful, and she'd kissed him on the cheek. And that was it. He'd never seen her again.

Jilly snapped her fingers in front of his eyes. "Earth to Linc. Did you hear me?"

He'd been too lost in his last memory of Nomi. "No. Sorry."

His sister rolled her eyes. "Focus. She's coming back, so what are you going to do about it?"

"Pick her up from the train station."

"Please don't be obtuse. This is your chance."

"She's only staying a couple of days, Jilly."

"I know, but that in itself is huge. She hasn't been home in five years. Maybe you can convince her to stay a little longer. Have a Christmas fling."

A fling? Just the thought made his skin tight. "Not that easy, Jilly. She's coming back for Nolan Polk."

Jilly's eyes grew wide and she cursed under her breath. "What are you going to do?"

That was the question. He'd created the Nolan Polk pseudonym for his work back in college when he'd been trying to distance himself from the family name. He'd wanted people to want his work because it was good, not because his father was a senator. But one bad decision and Polk had become a prison he couldn't escape.

There was no way in hell he could help her find Nolan Polk. Problem was, when Nomi had something she wanted, she wouldn't let it go.

"I can't use the Polk name or distribute that work

until the New Year. If I do, I'm in breach and it'll cost me everything."

Jilly ground her teeth. "I could kill that woman for locking you into this deal."

He wished he could wipe his whole relationship with Melanie Stanfield off the plane of existence. Just thinking about it made anger pulse in his veins. When he and Melanie had been together, at first things were great. She had art connections thanks to her family, particularly abroad. When he'd proposed, she'd officially become his manager.

The one clause in his contract he should have paid closer attention to stated that no one else could distribute his work for profit for a term of three years. At the time, he'd been convinced of their love. *Like a chump.*

But then things had gone bad. And she'd started paying more attention to the value of his work than the value of their relationship. When they'd broken up, she'd held him by the short and curlies to his contract. He'd rather eat glass than give her a dime.

For the past two years since he'd been home, he hadn't sold or exhibited a single piece, except for charity. Suddenly the only thing he'd ever wanted had a hundred-and-ten-pound blond albatross attached to it.

But he'd made his bed, he had to lie in it. "My fault, Jilly. I trusted the wrong person. I'm not eager to do that again."

Jilly shook her head. "Nomi wouldn't hurt you, Linc. That's not her."

No, that wasn't the Nomi he remembered, but he'd been wrong about people before. "I thought the same thing about Melanie once, too."

His sister put a hand on his shoulder. "Maybe this

gig could put you back on the map again. Have you shooting. This is your chance to finally leave for good. Maybe go back to Europe. See more of Africa. You always used to talk about it."

"That was a long time ago, Jilly."

She pursed her lips. "Sooner or later you won't have Dad as an excuse anymore. You'll have to face the big bad world. You were destined for great things, little brother. Time to stop hiding."

Linc ignored the numb feeling that spread from his chest. With his father's early-onset Alzheimer's diagnosis two years ago, he'd come home to help out. They both had. But for him, it had also been a way to escape all the mistakes he'd made.

Though, coming home hadn't been any easier. His father had been a man's man. Confident, a little brash, but fair and kindhearted. It had helped him get elected over and over again. It had helped people trust him. But that man was gone now. And it hurt. Some days weren't so bad. The lucid days. Which were more than the non-lucid days. But the other days, the ones where his father couldn't even recognize him, those hurt. It was the sole reason he stayed. Otherwise he'd have left, off for parts unknown by now, spreading his wings. At least that was what he liked to tell himself.

"You wouldn't understand."

"Whatever you say. What I do know is, all you have to do to get the girl of your dreams is to share a part of yourself. It's not that hard, Linc. Now's your chance to take a shot. Even if it's just for a couple of days."

"First things first. I need to keep Nomi from finding Nolan Polk. Then I'll worry about taking a shot." Too bad his brain and his heart had different priorities.

Chapter 3

It was official. Hell had frozen over. And it looked an awful lot like Faith, Virginia. Nomi strode through the train station looking around at the white canvas outside. Of course it was snowing. This was Virginia, after all, and there were only a few days left till Christmas. What had she expected? The balmy seventy-degree weather in Los Angeles looked mighty good right about now.

Get in and get out and you can go back.

She was giving herself three days to get what she needed and be back at home in the safety of her apartment before Christmas hit.

She turned on her phone and checked her messages. So far nothing from Linc. Hopefully he was already here. She was behind the curve as it was. Amber had used her miles to upgrade herself to an earlier flight and presumably had caught the afternoon train, so Nomi was playing catch up.

She took the escalator down, choosing to walk rather than ride it. All the while she scanned the luggage area for Linc. Frowning when she didn't see him, she craned her neck. *Don't be ridiculous. He might have changed in all this time.*

The last she'd seen him, his dark hair had dusted his shoulders and he'd been rail thin and barely taller than her at maybe five feet nine inches if she was being generous. She had no idea what to picture now. Maybe he'd gone extra emo like every other hipster she knew and had grown a beard or a mustache to be ironic.

As she looked around, the memories of the last time she'd been home washed over her. When she'd left here five years ago, the plan had been to never come back.

Thanks to her AP courses and the summer sessions she'd taken at the local community college, she'd finished all her high school credits just before the holiday and had planned to work from December through graduation and then head for UCLA in the fall. Brad was supposed to move out with her and had been planning on attending the University of Southern California. But that night had changed everything.

When he'd picked her up, he'd taken her to the big lake by the country club. Over the summers there were usually parties out there, bonfires on the tiny beach. It was also the standard make-out spot. But he hadn't taken her there to make out. Or, hell, propose like her idiotic seventeen-year-old self had thought.

Just thinking about what he'd said made her blood boil. "Nomi, it's been a fun two years, but we need to think about our futures. Or rather, I need to think about *my* future."

She'd been too shocked to cry in the moment. And since she hadn't said anything he'd continued.

"As great as you are, you're not the right person to take into my future. I need to be with someone who complements me. Someone who has the same vision."

What he'd meant was someone with a rich family and even richer connections. For the most part, his parents had been okay with her. His mother was more disapproving of her middle-class roots than the color of her skin. But she'd never missed an opportunity to parade rich, blonde debutants in front of Brad. The ass wipe had finally taken notice. His next words still sat with her today. "I'm seeing Lila Banks now."

She'd finally found her voice then. "Lila Banks? That wannabe socialite barely has one brain cell."

"Well, she's perfect and her family is perfect. And I also got into Georgetown. I think even you can agree that it's is a better school than USC. You don't really fit into my circles. And, let's face it, not everyone would understand our relationship. You're the only one who didn't see this coming."

"H-how long?" She'd never regretted a question more.

"A few weeks. I'd have told you sooner. But your dad, he implied my history grade would be in jeopardy if I hurt you." Nomi could still visualize his strong shoulders as they shrugged. "So I waited until after the report cards had been sent."

Even now, Nomi could remember the instant nausea when he'd said that. Her parents had known. They could have insulated her or protected her and they hadn't said a word. That verbal slap had left scars.

Brad had been with her as a note of rebellion, but now that real life was starting, he wanted his perfect blonde girlfriend and perfect life, and Nomi didn't fit. She'd walked away from him, leaving him at the top of the hill. Tears streaming down her face, she'd walked across the golf course and through the trails to Jilly's house. Somewhere along the way it had started to rain, the frozen splashes stinging her face as she walked.

Jilly hadn't been there. But Linc had. He'd opened the door and dragged her inside by the fire and wrapped a blanket around her. After a change of clothes, a go-around with Jilly's blow-dryer and some hot cocoa, she had felt better.

He hadn't asked her a thing, merely been there. Linc hadn't batted an eyelash when she had asked for a ride home so she could pack. His only objection when she had asked for a ride to the train station was that she should wait for Jilly to come back before she left. But her friend was at Villanova visiting the college, and Nomi wanted out so bad she couldn't wait.

She would never forget his last words to her. "You always deserved better than him."

Then he'd given her a hug and his phone number and told her to call him if she ever needed anything. And that was that. Before that, they'd only been peripheral friends. She'd always seen him just as Jilly's brother. But she'd always liked him. Unlike most of the other kids at her school, he'd talked to her when Brad wasn't around. Nothing heavy, but he always went out of his way to make her feel comfortable. She'd always assumed it was because her mom worked for his father, but given that he was braving the cold to come pick her up now, maybe he was just a nice guy.

When she didn't see him, she shuffled to the baggage claim wishing she'd worn her Uggs instead of her Cole Haan stiletto boots. She'd opted to check her bag instead of lugging it from car to car. Her train from Dulles had carried the usual commuter crowd, so the claims area was practically empty even though there were plenty of people waiting for their passengers.

For the most part, no one paid her any attention, but after several minutes the hairs on the back of her neck stood at attention. Nervously, she whipped around, expecting to see someone behind her. There was no one there. But at the far corner of the arrivals area, a man stared at her. He was tall, maybe around six feet or so. And he had one of those thin, rangy builds that screamed soccer player or some sort of athlete. His dark hair curled over his forehead and framed one hell of a face. *Holy hell.* There were men that hot in Faith? Maybe she'd been missing out.

Nervously she turned back and dragged her roll along off the luggage carousel.

Her neck still prickled with awareness. Oh jeez, was he staring? She hazarded another glance over her shoulder. This time when their eyes met, the corner of his lips tipped up in a hint of a smile and her insides flipped.

No. No. No. She was not getting distracted by some hottie. She had a job to do. Tall-dark-and-rip-your-clothes-off over there was a dime a dozen in Los Angeles. Granted, the ones in LA were also pompous ass hats for the most part.

She turned back around to keep from staring some more, pulled up Linc's contact info on her phone and sent a quick text. Hey, are you still okay to pick me up?

His reply came quickly. Yeah. I'm already here.

Her brows snapped down. Had she missed him? The station was slowly thinning out. Despite her brain's commands to not look at the guy in the corner, she couldn't help a furtive glance. He smiled at her then and something pulled low in her belly, making her ache.

Oh hell. She'd never been the one-night-stand type,

but for that smile, she'd give it some serious consid-
erations. *Focus, Nomi.* She turned her attention back
to her phone. Where are you? What are you wearing?

The suggestive nature of the text didn't hit her until
she'd already hit send. Aww hell. She'd been home all
of five minutes and she was already a hot mess.

He was slower to respond now. Dark jeans. Dark
jacket. And I'm waving.

This time she looked up and her jaw went slack. Tall-
dark-and-turns-good-girls-bad was waving.

Pushing off the wall, he sauntered over with one of
those panty-dropping smiles. As he got closer, Nomi's
heart hammered faster and faster; she was certain she'd
have a heart attack.

He paused just in front of her. "I guess you didn't
recognize me."

Still slack jawed, she stared up at him and catalogued
his face. His jade green eyes were dark and reminded
her of the forest after a heavy rainfall. The cleft in the
chin that had only been hinted at when they were kids
was more defined. His angled jaw and chiseled cheekbones, combined with full sensual lips, meant Lincoln
Porter had turned into a full-blown hottie.

*Speak. Close your mouth, swallow and then find
some intelligent words.* The brain's commands were
sound, but all she managed was, "Linc?"

He chuckled. "Yeah." He ran a hand over his hair.
"It's me. I guess I look a little different."

"Understatement of the year."

The smile was back. "How about we get out of here
and get you settled?"

Chapter 4

Nomi hadn't recognized him. What the hell was he supposed to make of that? Okay, fair enough—the summer before college he'd added three inches to his frame and packed on some muscle finally when he'd started doing parkour. His mother always said he'd grow into his looks. But he never expected Nomi to walk right by him.

More dangerously, he wanted to know what she thought. He'd seen her appraising gaze as it slid over him, but from a distance it was hard to tell.

She swallowed hard. "Sorry. You just look so…" Her voice trailed, but even in the bad lighting of the station, he could see her pupils dilate. With her lips parted ever so slightly, he wanted to take her photograph.

Yeah, not gonna happen. The moment she found out he was Nolan Polk, she'd take what she needed and bolt.

And he didn't want to go through that again. "It's good to see you, Nomi. You look good."

She wore her hair in slim braids that hung down her back. Her smile, now, that was the same. Her lips naturally curved upward, making her look as if she was always on the verge of laughter or mischief. She hadn't changed at all. Still slim, but her curves had filled in, making him itch to touch. Her cinnamon skin gleamed. And her wide, dark, almond-shaped eyes missed nothing.

She was still beautiful. *And likely still hung up on Brad Lennox, so get your mind right, Linc.*

He cleared his throat. "C'mon, let's go get you settled." She'd only packed a carry on so it was easy enough to take that from her and pull it along.

"Must we?" she mumbled under her breath.

Linc chuckled. Her acerbic wit was still intact. "I see you're no more fond of this place than when you left it."

Nomi shrugged. "I always knew you were astute."

Oh yeah, she hadn't changed. Problem was, he hadn't changed either, so she still had the power to make him a little nervous. "So if you hate it so much, then what are you doing back here? At Christmastime no less. Surely someone else could have come. I seem to recall you saying you'd rather have your fingernails torn out."

"Hey, the night is still young." With a small laugh she added, "Hopefully, I'll be in and out. If my career trajectory didn't depend on it, I wouldn't be here encroaching on your Christmas holiday."

Once at his BMW, he unlocked and opened the passenger door for her, then deposited her bag in the trunk before sliding behind the wheel.

"You're not encroaching, Nomi. I'm happy to help.

And since you won't be able to rent a car anywhere in a thirty-mile radius, I can take you anywhere you need to go." This situation wasn't ideal. The last thing he wanted her to do was find out he was Nolan Polk, at least until he was sure he could trust her. This way he could find out what she was really after.

She turned in her seat to study him. As her gaze slid over his face, he bit back the sudden compulsion to kiss her. She always had that unnerving way of looking at someone directly, clear to the soul.

"You seriously don't need to do that. I can manage."

"Independent to the bone. But be reasonable. You'll need help. I'm offering."

"I—" Nomi shook her head. "Honestly, I don't even know what I'm looking for. You'd be signing up for what amounts to a wild-goose chase."

There was no way he was letting her roam around asking questions. Not so much that he feared she'd actually find anything, but more that he wanted to keep her close. Maybe Jilly was right, and she was the same old Nomi, and he could trust her. But then maybe she cared more about her bottom line than anything else. The only way to know was to keep her close.

"Look, I get it. You like to do everything on your own. But help from a local can't be a bad thing."

"I don't want to keep you from anything. I'd feel terrible. And it's the holiday. I'm sure you have family obligations. A girlfriend. Somebody is going to need you. I got this."

His breathing slowed. Did she just ask if he had a girlfriend? "Right now *you* need me. Family is fine and no girlfriend. Why can't you just accept help?"

She ducked her head. "I guess I've never been very good at it. I'd rather count on myself."

Only with a Herculean effort did he manage to keep his gaze from flickering to her chest. "Can't have that, now, can we? Besides, my mother and Jilly would have my hide if I didn't help you. You're practically family." *Shit, way to put it out there.*

She blinked, then again. "Uh, whatever the reason, I appreciate it. And any return favor, just name it."

"Am I taking you to your parents' house?"

She shook her head vehemently. "God, no. I haven't seen either of them in a year, and birthday conversations were awkward enough without me being under their roof. Besides, I'm not staying for the holidays, so there's really no point of letting them know I'm here."

"So where to, if not your parents'?"

"Resplendence Inn," she said absently.

She was staying there? That was the most expensive hotel in town. Vacationing celebrities looking for a Norman Rockwell Christmas had put Faith on the map. The town had become a booming tourist destination, and with that had come development. Resplendence was one of the newer boutique hotels. "Nice place."

She shrugged. "The magazine booked it."

"So what exactly do you want Nolan Polk for?"

Her morose mood lifted the second she started talking about her job. "*Sassy* magazine is having their twentieth-anniversary issue and we're doing a women in beauty spread. But not like the usual bullshit stuff that the other magazines do featuring photoshopped celebrities who don't even look like that. Or just the western aesthetic. We wanted to capture real women around the world. This Polk guy, you should see his work. He does the most moving and intimate candid portraits. I think you'd like his stuff. You used to be into photography, if I remember correctly?"

Used to. "Yeah. I dabbled."

She narrowed her gaze. "You more than dabbled, from what I remember. Didn't you win a competition or two? I always thought you'd leave here and travel the world with your pictures."

And he had. Or at least that was before he'd had his heart ripped out and come home to lick his wounds. "Well, funny thing is, there is no place like home." The last thing he wanted was for her to dig further about him, so he changed the subject. "So what's going on? You lost your artist?"

"I didn't lose him, exactly. He just doesn't want to be found. Little does he know I don't give up on anything. Ever. And I need to find him before Amber does. If she finds him first and convinces him to give her a photo, then she gets my promotion."

"Who's Amber?"

"My nemesis who works at the magazine. She's in town looking for Nolan, too, and she's had a head start."

Damn, there was someone else looking for him? How was he supposed to keep two of them at bay? "So, what? You plan on finding him and convincing him to be part of this spread?"

"Short answer, yes. But more than that, I feel like I get him. I wish I could explain, but his photos, they do something to me. They make me feel something. I want him to know I understand him and that *Sassy* isn't going to exploit his work. I'm hoping that appeals to him. My job depends on it."

"You do have this way of manifesting what you want.

I mean, look at you. You always talked about working for a fancy magazine. And now you are."

Her gaze narrowed. "You remember that?"

"Just because you barely noticed me doesn't mean I didn't notice you." He pulled into the hotel's parking lot in front of the valet stand. Not giving her a chance to respond, he was out of the car quickly, pulling her luggage out of the trunk and beating the valet to her door to open it. He needed to stop blurting things out around her.

She accepted his proffered hand. "Thanks, Linc. I have it from here."

Yeah, he should probably just head home, but he wasn't ready to say good-night yet. "If it's just the same, I'll make sure you're settled in. Jilly would have my head if I didn't."

She silently studied him for a minute, then her gaze shifted to his mouth. Linc's heart tripped into full gallop. With their breath lingering between them in puffs of visible air, his blood hummed just under his skin. But then her gaze shifted away and the moment was gone.

He led her inside to the lobby and she shifted from foot to foot in her boots. "I don't even have the words to thank you."

"It was just a pickup from the train station. No big deal."

She winced. "Well, and helping me find Nolan Polk. I owe you."

Cocking his head, he said, "Let me just add that to your tab."

At check-in, she gave her name and the desk agent searched for her name. He took that time to drink in his fill of Nomi. Sure, he'd be seeing her a lot over the next couple of days, but he wanted the unfiltered Nomi, who didn't have her walls up.

"I'm sorry, Miss Adams, but your reservation was cancelled."

Nomi's head snapped up and she glared at the registration attendant. "Please check again. It was booked by *Sassy* magazine."

"I have, ma'am, and we have one reservation under that booking. A Miss Amber Divine. Your reservation was cancelled. This evening around four."

Nomi shook her head. "That's insane. I was on a flight at that time. Fine. Whatever, just rebook me." She clamped her hands together on the counter; she was the picture of calm, but he could sense the heat coming off her body.

"I'm sorry, we gave the reservation away."

"Excuse me—"

Linc placed a hand at the small of her back and her jaw snapped shut. Glancing at the attendant's name, he smiled, calling up whatever Porter charm he'd been blessed with. "Karen. I hope you realize the error you've made. Miss Adams is a guest of my family. Senator Porter would be disappointed if you couldn't resolve this problem. There must be something you can do."

Karen blinked rapidly. "Of—of course, Mr. Porter." But after another check through the VIP rooms, nothing was available.

Nomi hung her head. "I'll need to get a hold of Amber and room with her."

"No. You won't. I have another idea. Come with me," Linc said.

"Where are we going?"

"Trust me. I know of somewhere better than the Resplendence Inn."

"And you think they'll have rooms days before Christmas?"

"I can guarantee it."

Thirty minutes later, she was standing in the middle of one of the guesthouses on his family's property. "Linc, I don't even know what to say. You're really going above and beyond with this whole white-knight thing."

He shoved his hands into his pockets and rocked back on his heels. The smile she gave him was reminiscent of seventeen-year-old Nomi. There was no way he'd crack that shell if she left in a couple of days. He wanted to spend some time with her. "I know you said you'd owe me."

"Anything. If I have the power to give it to you, it's yours."

Oh boy. His brain conjured up images of her twined around his body naked in front of a fire, and he had to shake his head to get rid of the imagery that would likely drive him insane for weeks. "Go with me to Brad Lennox's wedding on New Year's Eve."

Her beautiful mouth fell open. "No way in hell."

He'd anticipated that response from her. "How about you sleep on it?"

"My answer's not going to change. Pick something else. *Anything* else."

He considered it. Hell, the way she parted her lips, he considered asking for a kiss instead. But the wedding bought him some time with her. "Tell you what, we'll talk about it tomorrow."

"Why are you being so stubborn?"

Because I want you. "Because you never come home, and I need a date."

She pursed her lips. "I'll still say no tomorrow."

Linc merely shrugged. "I'll take my chances.

Chapter 5

The next morning, Nomi tossed and turned in bed. Sexy Linc was *not* part of the bargain. Yes, he could help her, and yes, she needed him, but he was not supposed to look like he did. Nor was he supposed to ask her out to the one event she certainly couldn't go to.

And she certainly was not supposed to respond to him like that. Just thinking about his intense, focused green eyes on her made her feel flushed.

Over the past five years she'd dated some, but nothing serious. After all, her last serious relationship had sent her fleeing her home under the cover of darkness, so she was more than a little gun shy. And the guys she had dated were nice enough, some with great potential, but she had yet to meet a guy who gave her that same kind of exhilarating rush that her job did. So she just didn't bother.

The knock on her door came at eight sharp and she

was a little surprised to find Linc on the other side. They weren't supposed to meet until eight thirty. "Oh, good morning. I'm almost ready. I just need to finish my makeup."

"Sorry I'm early, but I figured maybe we could get breakfast before we head over to Jilly's gallery. Besides, she'll kill me if I don't bring her a pastry from Claire's bakery."

Nomi smiled. "I see Jilly still has her sweet tooth. How is she doing anyway?" Nomi shoved aside the twinge of guilt. She didn't want to ask secondhand, but Jilly would pretend she was okay for Nomi's sake. Her fiancé had called off their wedding in New York just six months ago and Jilly'd had a rough time.

"You know Jilly. She's tough."

"She also puts on a brave face even when she shouldn't."

He gave her that almost smile of his again. The man was dangerous to her equilibrium. "Like someone else I know."

She raised her brow. "You're her twin, so if anyone would know, I suppose it would be you."

"She's still hurt and reeling. But she's good. She's back at work and business is booming. Jilly will bounce back. She always does."

She put down her powder brush. "I was sad to hear about your father. How's he doing?"

Linc shrugged "Fine, I guess. It's hard to see him slipping, you know. Most days he's lucid and he wants to work. But there are days now where he's not even sure where he is and who people are. It's killing Mom."

"Can't be easy on you, either."

Again he avoided talking about his father, this time

by changing the subject. "After the gallery, do you know where you might want to try next?"

Guilt pricked at her. He had enough things to worry about without shuttling her around town. "What about work?"

"I work at the winery for Mom. I'm the operations director."

"I'm sure she needs you."

He rolled his eyes. "Everything is shut down until after the holiday. I'm all yours."

The way he said that sent a tingle through her body, awakening nerve endings she hadn't thought about in a very long time.

"I feel bad. I'm sure there are things you'd rather be doing than spending every waking minute with me."

His gaze skimmed over her body. "Not really. How about this? I'll feed you, take you to see Jilly and we'll see where things are. It probably won't be easy to find this guy, especially if he doesn't want to be found and it's tourist season."

She nodded. "Yeah, okay. I just wanted to get this done as quickly as possible so I can get out before the holiday."

He cocked his head. "Not a fan at all of Christmas?"

"Yeah, well, I've been soured on the whole holiday season."

"That's a shame. No eggnog, no caroling, no presents?"

Nomi laughed. "Hold up now. I still like presents. I'm not an idiot."

He nodded, his eyes narrowing imperceptibly. "Lennox really did a number on you."

No. She was not discussing Brad Lennox. "He's not

even on my radar. I'm here to work and get out of Faith as fast as my stilettos can carry me. And I'm sorry, Linc, but you'll have to think of another way to have me pay you back. I slept on it, and I still can't go to his wedding with you."

His lips tipped up at the corners. "We'll talk about it later. Right now, your taxi service awaits."

She had a sinking suspicion he wasn't going to let it go. But she was hungry and needed fuel for that kind of fight.

For breakfast he took her somewhere she'd never been, just on the outskirts. Even though it was still somewhat early, the place was full of tourists, but at least there wasn't a line out the door. If this were LA, there would be at least an hour wait.

While they waited for their food, she studied him. "You know, I realize I don't know you that well. Even back then, I didn't really *know* you. All I know is you run an excellent taxi service and you were sweet enough to offer a girl a lifeline when she needed one."

His laugh transformed his face, making him appear more open and, if possible, more handsome. The sound rolled over her, making her warm from the inside out despite the chill outside. "I'm an open book. Ask me anything you want to know."

She widened her eyes. "Anything? You realize that as a journalist, my whole job is to ferret out the story I'm looking for. This is a dangerous proposition for you."

"I think I can take it."

"Don't say I didn't warn you. No evading, Porter. You have to answer honestly."

He shifted in his seat a little, but his gaze never wavered from hers. "Do your worst. Just remember, turnabout is fair play."

She weighed her options. She had no life to speak of besides the magazine, so he could ask her whatever he wanted. "Fine."

He leaned back to make room for the waitress bringing them their coffee. "Shoot."

She opened her mouth, but decided to take a sip of coffee first. Sighing in contented bliss, she put her cup back down. When she looked at him again, he was staring at her, his green eyes now hot and dark.

"What?"

"That look on your face. It's sexy."

She blushed, but would put down money saying he couldn't see it. "I see you're starting with the flattery."

"Or truth." He shrugged.

Nomi laughed. This felt like…flirting. *Or maybe you're woefully out of practice.* "You were super smart. I figured you'd go off to law school or something, like the rest of the prep school set, or bum around Europe. What are you doing back in Faith?"

He opened his mouth, then a light flush stained his cheeks, but he answered her. "I did all that. Transferred every AP credit I could and busted my ass to graduate from Carnegie Mellon in three years. Travelled some, came home. Not much to the story."

"Now, why don't I believe you?"

Her flashed her another grin. "I did graduate from CMU. Have the diploma to prove it."

"You know what I mean." She changed tactics. "You could do anything. Go anywhere, be with anyone. Why here?"

"Dad got sick, and the way I figure it, there's plenty

of time for me to go do other things. Mom has needed more help at the winery."

"Are you happy?"

A shadow drifted across his face, but then his good-natured smile was back in place. "Right in this moment, yeah. Good food in the company of a beautiful woman."

Her heart rate picked up in response. *Easy does it. We're here to work. Not flirt.* For the rest of breakfast, she kept things on safer topics—catching up on some of the people she'd known, local gossip, her job and their favorite places to travel.

He relaxed her and made it easy to forget where she was, but a flash of red hair outside the window was all the reminder she needed. *Amber.* She was going somewhere in a hurry, and Nomi didn't have time to sit here on a leisurely breakfast date. "I see my competition is already up and at 'em. Do you think we can head to Jilly's now?"

He made a poor attempt at hiding his smile. "Sure, let me get the check."

"Oh, I can't let you do that. You're doing me the favor, remember?"

"I insist. I'll add it to your tab. Why don't you get the car warmed up."

While he flagged down the waitress, she headed out to start the car. She climbed into the passenger seat of the SUV and leaned over to stick the key in the ignition. Maybe if she'd been more alert, better mentally prepared, or hadn't wasted part of the morning pretending she was on a bed-and-breakfast date, she would have noticed the woman coming out of the post office four doors down.

With her smooth chocolate skin and high cheekbones, she was the picture of Nomi in another twenty years. Nomi froze, not sure what to do. She hadn't called her parents and hadn't planned to. But still, she couldn't ignore the twinge of pain in her heart at seeing her mother again.

Adrenaline spiking through her blood, Nomi knew she had to make a decision. If she didn't move, then her mother would see her.

For several loud, pulsing heartbeats, she stayed like that, but then her brain kicked in. Just as her mother was about to look up from her bag, Nomi ducked. She'd call home. Just not right now. *Later.* Maybe tonight. Maybe tomorrow. Definitely before she left…*maybe.*

The driver's door swung open and Linc laughed. "What are you doing?"

Sheepish, she sat up. "I, uh, thought I lost an earring."

His brows rose. "Did you find it?"

"Yep." She pointed at her ear. "Put it right back." She could tell that he didn't believe her, but she did not want to get into some long conversation about why she was hiding from her mother.

By the time they reached Jilly's gallery, she felt more at ease. Linc's sister had always been exuberant. It was no wonder she'd been a part of the pep squad at school. "Nomi! It's so good to see you." She bounded up to her and enveloped her into a warm hug.

Nomi squeezed back and let herself settle into the feeling of being home. She'd missed Jilly. Her bestie had been out to LA frequently to see her, or they'd met in places like New York, DC or San Francisco.

"Oh my God, Nomi, you have to tell me everything. Start talking. I'm so sorry I couldn't be there yesterday, but Linc came to the rescue, right? He wasn't late, was he?"

"No, Linc was perfect." Damn, why did her voice sound so husky? She cleared her throat. "I didn't recognize him at first."

"He's changed a lot, huh? Sometimes I can't even believe it. You would think he'd have a girlfriend, but for some strange reason he doesn't. If you ask me, he's carrying a torch for someone."

Linc's brows rose, then he coughed. "Enough, Jilly."

Nomi resisted the urge to shiver while she glanced between brother and sister, trying to figure out what the sudden note of tension was about. "Jilly, we have so much to catch up on."

Her friend squeezed her hand. "We will find a way to make time before you go, okay? In the meantime, I know you didn't come all this way for a snow fix. What do you need?"

"Even if it's at midnight. We'll figure it out. So, your gallery has showed some work of one of my favorite photographers."

Jilly nodded, understanding. "Nolan Polk."

"Is there anything you can tell me about him? What he looks like? Any places he might frequent? Even better, where he lives? It's important I get a hold of him."

Jilly bit her lip. "Have you tried his agent? She might know how to reach him best."

Nomi rolled her shoulders. "Yes, repeatedly. I've tried everything. I keep getting the 'Mr. Polk doesn't take unsolicited requests' message. I'm sort of desperate. We're looking to put his photographs in our twentieth-anniversary issue featuring beauty around the world. I think some of the portraits he's done around the world would be ideal."

"Well, he is extremely talented. No doubt about that. But unfortunately, I can't tell you much about him."

There was something about the way Jilly slid her gaze away when she said that. "Look, I get it. You're protecting your relationship with him. But anything you can tell me would be helpful. What does he like, where might I look next? I'm sort of running out of time."

Jilly slid a glance toward her brother and sighed. "Okay, fine. First place you might look is Faith Woods. He used to do a lot of photos out in the woods. Rumor is he has a cabin there. Then tomorrow night, there's an auction at the country club. Every year for the past three years, he's donated a piece. I doubt he'll be there, but it's worth a shot."

The country club? One of the last places she wanted to go. But if it meant a chance at Nolan Polk, then she'd better pull out her little black dress. But first, she and Linc were going to the woods.

Chapter 6

This was insane and Linc knew it. But, as he was quickly learning, there was no deterring Nomi from something she wanted to do. She was too damn stubborn.

"You know, you didn't have to drive me."

He slid her a glance. "Yes, I did." It was the only way to keep her out of trouble. "The roads are a mess out here from the last snow, and you don't actually have a car, so what were you going to do, walk?"

"If it meant getting here ahead of Amber, then yes."

"What is the competition thing with that girl anyway?"

Nomi sighed and wiped away the fog on the passenger side window. "She's hated me since I started at *Sassy.*"

He would never understand the dynamics between women. "Girl jealousy bullshit?"

She shrugged. "Something like that. I know I can come off a little strong, but she hated me on sight."

"You? Come on strong?" he teased. That earned him a shove in the shoulder.

"I know I'm driven and that puts people off."

"I dunno. I think it's sexy. You know what you want and nothing stands in your way." It also scared the shit out of him, because if anyone could find Nolan Polk, it was *her*. Hell, they were *here*, at *his* cabin.

So stupid. He couldn't risk her knowing who he was just yet. His contract with Melanie was up in a little over a week. He had that long to determine if Nomi could be trusted. If she hung around that long.

He couldn't wait to live his life again without Melanie clouding every decision he made. That was if he even felt like picking up a camera. It had been months. Though, sitting here with Nomi, with the sunlight streaking in, highlighting the reddish tones in some of her braids, he itched to capture it.

Her laugh was low and throaty. "You would be the only man on the face of the earth that finds my relentlessness sexy. Sometimes I feel like I repel guys. It's okay, though. I'm about to be the youngest senior editor in the history of the magazine if I can pull this off."

His gut clenched. The way she said it—as if it was the thing that would make her whole life—a part of him wanted to give it to her. "I think you're wrong, but it's a moot point. Anyway, we're here."

She sighed. "It's kind of peaceful."

"Don't tell me the city slicker girl is missing her small hometown."

"Don't get it twisted, I *love* the city. The hustle and bustle. Los Angeles has a way different energy than

Virginia does. But I do like my quiet moments. It must be easy to be creative out here with all the solitude. Nothing to do but listen to your imagination."

It was peaceful. That was why he liked it. He could get away from the noise and just be himself. Granted, he hadn't been here in a while. No need.

Nomi opened her door and a gust of icy wind blew in, chilling him to the bone. Right about now, LA didn't sound so bad. He'd never been. An added bonus—Nomi lived there. *Sap.*

He followed her up the front stairs of the cabin, her tight ass sashaying in front of him in her leggings. She'd tossed the impractical boots she'd worn yesterday, and opted for flat ones with sheep's wool lining.

Nomi knocked on the door and waited as patiently as she could. After only a brusque knock, she was peering into the windows.

He ignored the twinge of guilt. He knew no one was coming. "Looks like no one is home."

She tsked at him. "Linc, you give up way too easily. Where is your determination?" She hopped down the stairs and started around the back.

"Where are you going? You need to be careful." He could only imagine how pissed she'd be if she slipped on some ice and twisted an ankle.

"I'm fine. I'm not some west coast rube who's never seen snow or ice before."

"Still, it's a long time since you've been here, Nomi."

She shrugged. "Last I checked the stuff doesn't change. Cold, slippery, wet."

"Suit yourself." He couldn't help the smile as she had to check her balance more than once.

At the back of the house, she looked inside the windows again, then frowned. "I don't see anything."

"Nomi, the guy's not home."

"Yeah, but maybe he's fallen down and can't get up and he needs our help. Listen." He stilled and she added. "You can almost hear him calling out."

He rolled his eyes. "You're ridiculous."

"Surprisingly not the first time I've been told that." She scooted around him. "Come on, I need a better view of the whole place."

Linc stared at her. "You can't break in." Not to his place she couldn't. "Nomi!"

Her laugh rang from around the corner. "Relax, I'm not breaking in. Think of me as more of a Peeping Tom."

He joined her at the side of the house and cursed. She was trying to climb a stack of slippery logs to look inside. Linc stepped up behind her and dragged in a breath of chilly air. *I'm just giving her a lift. No need to get all excited. It's only for a second.* The problem was getting his hands on her was all he could think about.

Nomi looked over her shoulder. "What's the matter? I swear, I only want to have a quick look around. See if there's any indication he's been here or if this is even his cabin."

Linc knew she wouldn't find anything. He'd paid Hanna, the owner of Faith Woods Cabins, for a cellar to be added. Hell, he'd even brought in the crew and paid for all the work as a donation so he'd have somewhere to store all his equipment and files. "Fine, let's get this over with."

It wasn't the safest move in the world to touch her since it was all he'd been thinking about since he'd picked her up from the train station. He might not be able to stop.

Nomi planted her hands on the sill and he hoisted

her up easily. She might have been tall, but she didn't weigh much. And, added bonus, she smelled heavenly. Like chocolate and something else. Something spicier. He gritted his teeth. All he had to do was not breathe in. "Do you see anything?"

"No," Nomi panted. "Freaking nothing. For a photographer, there isn't a single camera lying around, or even a photo. No photography books, no nothing."

"Maybe we have the wrong cabin. Or maybe he was never a guest here at all." He hated the disappointment he heard in her voice. A snake of guilt slithered over his skin.

"I'm starting to think I'm on a wild-goose chase." She sighed. "Okay, coming down."

It would have been an easy task to bring her down slowly. *Should* have been. It would have been no big deal. *Should* have been no big deal. It should have been simple. *Should* have been. But she let go of the windowsill and her shift in weight unsettled them.

Next thing he knew they were falling backward and Nomi gave a little squeak of surprise. Linc wrapped his arms around her and cradled her inward to protect her body as he landed on his back on the snow-packed grass. His teeth clinked together as he took the brunt of their fall.

"Oh my God, Linc. Are you okay?"

He did a quick mental check as his teeth rattled and a jolt of adrenaline spiked his blood. His back had a residual ache he'd likely feel for days. But for the most part, he could feel all his fingers and toes. He was fine. Except...Nomi was now plastered against his body. Her ass nestled right in his lap. He wasn't sure if he was in heaven or hell—either way, his body loved it.

Chapter 7

Nomi wanted to melt into the molten heat surrounding her body. Relax into it and nestle there forever. Except she couldn't. Linc was the source of the heat, and right now, she was on his lap.

He sat up abruptly, bringing her with him, and she gasped. Through his jeans and her leggings, she could feel the insistent pulse of an erection. A very large erection. *Shit*.

Behind her, a wall of muscle braced her upright. In her attempt to scramble up, all she managed to do was rub against him, making her pulse quicken and her breath hitch as heat pooled between her thighs.

Linc planted both hands on her hips, his voice low and gravely as he squeezed gently. "Stop moving, Nomi." He sounded like warm whiskey on a cold night. She stilled.

"W-what?" She could barely force the two brain cells she had left to cooperate enough for speech.

"It'll be easier if you let me pick you up."

Right. "Oh."

Gently, he lifted her and set her next to him on the grass.

Despite the cold of the grass and the whipping air, Nomi flushed. Not only did Lincoln Porter have the devil's tempting smile but apparently, he had the power to turn her bones to liquid too.

Just having him hold her on his lap was enough to make her brain conjure all sorts of interesting scenarios about him naked. Nomi cleared her throat in an attempt to dissipate the imagery. What was she supposed to say? "I couldn't help noticing you were working with some serious equipment. Can I help you with that?" *No.*

She wasn't here looking for a fling. She was here for work. And Linc was doing her a favor. He didn't want her, current erection notwithstanding. She had pretty much given the poor man a lap dance.

Lucky for her, he took all the fumbling words out of her mouth and stood smoothly before extending a gloved hand to her. Swallowing hard, she placed her hand into his. When he spoke, his voice was low. "Tell me, Nomi, are you done with your adventures in B and E now?" He pulled her to her feet easily.

"Yeah. It's clear he's not here. If he ever was to begin with."

He watched her with those intense eyes of his and she shifted on her feet under the weight of his scrutiny. "You giving up on me?"

She lifted her chin. "Nope. There's still the auction tomorrow night."

His smile was fleeting. "There's the Nomi we all know and love. Come on, let's head into town."

The drive back to town carried an undercurrent of tension. None from Linc's side apparently, as he chatted with her about happenings in town.

But *she* felt the tension. Every time he touched her. Every time he slanted a grin at her. It was damned inconvenient.

After three more hours searching through the town and a false trail with his post office box, followed by coming up empty-handed with Jilly's contact at the bank, she was losing hope. Her feet hurt. Her back hurt. And to make matters worse, she was still hyper aware of Linc.

He pulled into the guesthouse entrance and she was surprised to find a car in the driveway. One she recognized. Her mother's.

She came out the back entrance before Linc had a chance to even park. Whistling low, he said, "You want me to stay with you?"

Nomi shook her head. She couldn't hide forever. Eventually she'd have to deal with her parents and now seemed as good a time as any. "No, I got it."

They both climbed out of his car and he headed straight for his room and she for her mother. Her mother's no-nonsense stride hadn't changed in the five years Nomi had been gone.

"Nomi Adams, do you want to explain to me how you come to town and you don't even tell your parents?"

She sighed. "I'm sorry. This was supposed to be a really quick trip."

"Nomi," her mother admonished.

Nomi clenched her jaw. She hated that tone. Hated how it made her feel like a misbehaving teenager. Never mind that she'd called her mother weeks ago and had yet to get a call back. But she hadn't come to fight, and no doubt Linc and his mother in the main house could hear them. "I'm sorry. I came for work. I should have come by the house. I didn't think it through."

"That's an understatement. Is that why you were hiding from me in the parking lot this morning?"

Damn, she'd seen her. "I wasn't hiding, exactly." She sighed and opted for a little honesty. "I panicked. If I'd had my way I wouldn't have even come back to Faith. And seeing you was sort of a shock to my system."

Her mother added more quietly, "When do you leave?"

"I'm not sure actually. I still haven't finished what I came to do."

"Why would you come stay with the Porters when you could have come home?"

What? And have them on her case all the time about how she never came home and how they couldn't possibly make it out to California for some reason or another? Her mother had spent her career following Senator Porter around, but now she claimed she didn't like to travel. They'd only been to see her twice. "It's a long story. The hotel was overbooked and Linc helped me out."

"You could have come home." Her mother softened her voice. "Since you're here and the holiday is only a few days away, you should come to dinner, see your father. Christmas Day?"

"I…" The last thing she wanted to do was go home. But she didn't want to do the same thing she accused them of. "If I'm still here, I'll come."

Her mother squared her shoulders. "I know it hasn't been easy. But we haven't seen you in a year and you haven't been home in ages. It will be good for all of us, don't you think?"

What she thought was that it might be torture. But there was no way out. Apparently, coming back to Faith also meant going home.

Chapter 8

The following night at the auction, after a fruitless day of searching, Nomi was tense. After last night's show-down with her mother, it was bound to happen. But when she located the Polk piece for auction, all the tension rolled out of her body. Normally, she was down for a fancy party. The auction was just part of the itinerary for this event. But tonight, even the nicest champagne wasn't making her any happier.

It was a beautiful portrait of what looked like north-ern China or possibly Mongolia. Several children were playing in the snow. Their chubby faces were framed by fur and their wide smiles were the universal kid lan-guage of 'this is so fun.' The one that he'd focused on, her eyes were a clear, bluish gray. And while she mostly looked like every other child there, she was clearly bi-racial.

Nomi stared for a long moment before whispering

to Linc. "It's gorgeous. You know, I've poured over his work for months and it always takes my breath away. Like he captures the essence of his subject's soul or something."

Next to her, Linc watched her carefully. "I guess you really like his work?"

She laughed. "Oh, come on, Linc, you were a photographer once. How can this beauty escape you?"

"It doesn't. Every one of his pieces that I see breaks my heart just a little. I feel like I know that little girl in the photo and her wool-covered hands and the joy she feels at playing in the snow." He cleared his throat. "I just like watching your reaction to his work."

"I appreciate beauty. What can I say?" The way he stared at her made her shift from foot to foot. "Let's go find Mr. Polk."

After a dead end with the auctioneer and a peek at the guest list to see who had arrived and checked in, Nomi had to swallow her disappointment. Nolan Polk wasn't there and he wasn't coming. Thanks to Ella, she knew he'd never actually made an appearance at any of these events, even in Faith, where he lived. The auctioneer told them he'd called in one year but that was it. He never attended. Damn, the man was slippery. Almost as if he knew she was looking for him and deliberately avoided her.

She'd left Linc inside greeting guests of the party while she got some air. *Think, Nomi, think. If I was a reclusive photographer, where would I hide?* Certainly not Faith, but that was just her.

The one consolation was that Amber hadn't found him, either. Nomi had seen her competition hovering at the edge of the auction talking to one of the guests.

It shouldn't bother her so much that Amber was here, but she knew the only reason the redhead was doing this was to get under her skin. It wasn't as if Amber was a real fan of Polk's work.

"Penny for your thoughts?"

Nomi whirled around to find Linc directly behind her. "Damn it, only ninjas should walk that softly."

He smirked. "What is it they say? Walk softly and carry a big—"

Nomi barked out a laugh. "*And* we have a comedian."

He shrugged. "Who said I was joking?"

The way Nomi talked about his work, Linc knew she understood it. *Or you just want to believe she understands it.* He wasn't fooling anybody. Least of all himself. He wanted to believe in Nomi because he wanted her. And that was a dangerous mix.

Like Melanie, she was super focused on her job, and getting to him was her objective. Once she got what she wanted, she wouldn't be interested in Linc the man, and he at least wanted a shot with her before he told her.

Her smile was slow. "Lincoln Porter, you realize it sounds like you're flirting with me."

"That's because I am." The Christmas fairies had also done him a favor. He nodded up at the mistletoe. "You're standing under mistletoe."

She snapped her head up. "Of course I am."

"Did you know that it's years of bad luck if you avoid a kiss under the mistletoe?"

Her laugh was soft, lilting. "It's funny, I hadn't heard that before."

Linc stepped into her space and she didn't back away.

Instead, she stood her ground and met his gaze. A smile tugged at his lips even as he dipped to kiss her.

The soft brushing of their lips sent a bolt of electricity through his body, and his body buzzed at the contact. When she parted them on a gasp, he groaned.

Sliding a hand up to cup her face, he deepened the kiss, angling her head so he could get better access. Her body slowly softened and molded against his as she reached her hands up to his lapels and drew him closer.

With his body snugly fitted against her, Linc couldn't think. She tasted like cinnamon and eggnog and home. Sweet and spicy, her full lips were so soft.

When her tongue slid over his, he groaned low in his throat and backed her up against the post. His erection kicked against her thigh and Nomi rotated her hips ever so slightly. The motion allowed him to slide a leg between hers, bunching up the skirt of her dress and bringing her heated core in contact with his thigh.

The blood rushed in his head and rational thought escaped him. Her scent swirled around him, fogging up his brain. When Nomi's hands slid into his hair, she tugged him closer, helping him deepen the kiss.

Linc slid his free hand from her waist to her ribcage and Nomi gasped into his mouth. With fire in his veins, he traced each of her ribs until his thumb traced the underside of her breast. Her hips rocked into his leg and he fought the pulsing wave of need that begged him to drag her out of there and get her horizontal.

A crash from behind them had them jumping apart. His heart thudding, he dragged his attention away from her, then back. Her dark eyes were wide with shock and surprise, but need still lingered.

Nomi blinked rapidly, as if trying to bring her brain

online, and when she did, she stepped out of his grasp. "You are very dangerous."

"I've been dying to do that for seven years, so I had to make it count." The words were out of his mouth before he could stop them.

But it was what she said next that really surprised him. "You should have done that a lot sooner."

Chapter 9

This was not part of the plan. But with the electricity and need humming through her veins, Nomi wasn't complaining, even though her mind reeled. How had she not known?

He tugged on her hand gently. "Look, Polk is a no-show. I have a surprise for you if you'll come with me."

She slid a glance toward the party. Amber was working the room. Maybe she should, too. But for the first time, work wasn't the only thing on her mind.

"Where are you taking me?"

Linc cocked his head. "You're choosing to come with me instead of staying?"

Nomi licked her bottom lip. She could still taste him, and his woodsy cologne wove an intoxicating web around her. She already had to stay in Faith longer than she thought. She could begin her search in the morning. "Well, when you kiss a girl like that, you leave no room for argument."

His wide grin was enough to stun her into silence. "Come on, I think you'll have fun. And don't worry, I'll help you find Polk. Tomorrow is Christmas, but we'll hit the pavement hard the day after."

She sighed and slid her hand into the warmth of his. "I have to admit, he's more slippery than I thought." *And* the reminder that tomorrow was Christmas made her stomach knot.

"We'll find him." His voice pitched lower. "I'll make sure you get what you're looking for, I promise."

"You shouldn't make promises you can't keep."

He merely winked at her.

"Maybe that will be my Christmas present." She looked up. "You hear that, Santa? I know we don't talk often, but I think I'm due."

Linc's laughter was rich. "Somehow I don't think that's how it works."

"What?" Nomi blinked innocently. "I can't just make demands of Santa Claus?"

"No, but come on, your surprise awaits." His smile turned mischievous, and Nomi's breath caught.

Jesus, his smile made her stomach do flips. "What *is* this surprise of yours?"

"I can't tell you. I'll have to show you. If you're up for it."

If she was— "Is that a dare?"

He shrugged. "Maybe. I mean, you've been living out in Cali with the palm trees and surfer boys. Maybe you've gone soft."

"Soft? Mr. Porter. You should know better than to dare me. Whatever you bring on, I can take."

He nodded as his gaze slid over her body. "In that case, we'd better get you changed."

Thirty minutes later, after a stop back at the house for her to don warmer clothes, they pulled up to the lake and Nomi laughed. "Ice-skating? You're kidding." Every winter the city cordoned off part of the lake for skating.

He grinned. "What? You're too good to ice-skate? Or is that the fear talking?"

How long had it been since she'd been out on the ice? It felt like a lifetime. Certainly not since she'd left. But when she was younger, it had been a tradition. Every teenager she'd known had been dragged out here for a date or two. It was a popular spot for its fire pits and seclusion. "I'm not scared. You should be, though. I used to be quite good."

"Fighting words. I like it."

He pulled a pair of skates out of the trunk and handed them to her. "Jilly said these should fit you. A size 8.5?"

He'd asked Jilly for help? The thought made her flush. Why had she never paid any attention to him before? Maybe if she hadn't been so blinded by Brad, then she would have seen how great he was then.

They laced their skates and he preceded her onto the ice, holding out a hand for her. She stared at it dubiously but Linc merely waited for her patiently. "Trust me. I'll make sure you don't fall." She placed her hand in his. "See. Was that so hard?" he asked.

"No, I guess not. It has been years since I've been ice-skating."

Linc led her around the ring easily. There were a few other skaters braving the cold. His voice was low when he asked, "Do you miss this place at all?"

She sighed. "When I left, I promised myself I wasn't coming back. I don't think I let myself miss it."

His hand tightened around hers. "Brad was an asshole, but this is your home."

"*Was* my home. I love Los Angeles."

"It seems to suit you."

"It does."

"Did you and your mom work things out?"

She blew a wayward braid out of her face. "Don't remind me. I'm supposed to be there for dinner tomorrow."

"Want me to come with you?"

She gaped at him. "You would do that?"

"Sure, why not? Besides, I like your mom. She was the best chief of staff Dad ever had."

"I've asked enough of you, don't you think?"

He shook his head. "It's no big deal. Besides, my mom will host her Christmas cocktails at ours as usual and I could use a date. We could go to your parents' house after." He was silent for a minute. "You ever going to give me an answer about the wedding?"

Nomi groaned. "Yes to drinks. It would be nice to see your parents again, especially as they are hosting me. But can't I repay you some other way? I really don't want to go to that wedding."

His voice was soft when he asked, "Do you still have residual feelings for him?"

"No. Hell no. I just don't want to see that crowd again. Zero desire." She slid a glance toward him and his disappointment was clear. "You really want me as your date?"

"I wouldn't have asked if I didn't."

She couldn't believe what she was about to say, but she owed him. She'd picked up a thank-you present for him in town yesterday. And she hoped it would really convey how grateful she was. Because saying yes didn't seem like enough. "Fine."

"Are you serious?"

"I can't believe it, but yeah, I guess I am. But only for you and Jilly am I staying in this godforsaken town another few days."

Linc picked her up and twirled her around. "Thank you."

"Don't thank me yet. There is a possibility I could still bolt with my hair on fire." Changing the subject, she said, "I remember you used to have pictures in your room of all these places you wanted to travel and see."

He was silent for several minutes. The only sound between them the slicing of their blades on ice. "For a while. I was that guy—have passport, will travel. But then things changed."

"Your mom needed you?"

"She did then. But not so much now. She's got a great support system. Lots of help."

"But you still stay?"

He shrugged. "It's home, Nomi."

"Do you still take photos?"

Linc swallowed hard as he shook his head. "I guess you could say I lost interest."

"That's too bad."

"I've had other things on my mind."

"That you have." Sliding a glance up at him, she finally asked him the one thing she'd been dying to since his lips left hers. "So, given that kiss, I take it you're not seeing someone?"

His grin flashed. "It's a safe bet to say no."

"How come? Clearly you come in some very nice packaging."

A laugh started deep in his belly and rumbled out. "Oh, you think so?"

She flushed. It was way too easy being with him. Felt too good. "Fishing for compliments, Lincoln?"

He plastered a hand to his chest. "Who, me?"

"Can't avoid my question." She laughed. "Why no one special for you?"

He raked his teeth over his bottom lip. "There was someone once. It didn't work out."

"Why?"

He sighed. "For starters, we were young. Then, well, she didn't really want me for me. She wanted a piece of me, or rather my name. So that wasn't going to work."

She frowned as she studied him. "I'm sorry. Clearly it's her loss. She probably regrets taking you for granted."

"I don't know. And I don't care." He twirled her toward the hot-chocolate stand and helped her off the ice. Once they'd ordered, he asked the one thing he'd been dying to know. "What about you? Anyone special since Brad?"

Nomi shook her head. "Nope."

"Oh, come on. You're gorgeous and fun. Add in there sexy as hell and smart as a whip, and most guys I know would be beside themselves trying to get your attention."

Nomi blinked up at him, unsure of what to say, so she took a sip of her hot chocolate to buy time. The moment the sweet, decadent chocolate hit her tongue, she moaned. He drew her in for a quick kiss and Nomi's heart stuttered. The moment his warm lips brushed over hers like satin, she shivered. He moaned low in his throat and relaxed her slowly.

"Sorry. I've been thinking about doing that since we left the party."

She blinked up at him even as she struggled to find the words. "You have a way of surprising a girl."

He laughed. "You can't be surprised that I'm attracted to you."

"It's not that. You just never seemed to pay me much attention back in high school."

He kissed her again softly and he tasted like hot chocolate. "Oh, I noticed you. You just weren't paying attention to *me*. I spent a lot of time staring at you. Whenever you came to the house to hang with Jilly, it was the sweetest torture in the world. I had all these elaborate scenarios in my head of how you'd kick Brad to the curb and you'd go out with me."

What? "How come you never said anything?"

"You were with Brad. It was like you didn't see anyone else. Besides…" He shrugged. "You were out of my league."

He had to be kidding. "I obviously made a mistake with Brad, then. I have a habit of not picking the best guys. When I started at the school, he sort of swooped in and just took over. Like I was an inevitability. I always hated that. But I don't think I was smart enough to really see him for what he was back then."

"An asshole."

Nomi laughed. "I see there's no love lost."

Linc rolled his shoulders. "He was a dick. Poked at me whenever he could. I think it chapped his ass that I was even allowed in the cool kids' clique."

Nomi rolled her eyes. "I know I was heartbroken at the time, but I dodged a bullet."

"Yeah you did."

"So if you don't really like him, then what are you doing going to his wedding?" She asked.

Linc's lips pressed then momentarily. "I'm standing in for Dad. He was invited. Well, he and my mother really. Since Mom has been looking after my father, she doesn't really do the social things that used to be an integral part of her schedule."

"That's understandable."

He shrugged. "Jilly and I stand in for them usually."

"Why aren't you taking Jilly to the wedding then?"

His smile was slow and dangerous. "Because I'd rather be going with you."

Chapter 10

At the end of the night, Nomi paused at her door, unsure of where this was going to end. Of where she wanted it to end. "Thank you for tonight. For all of today and yesterday really. It was fun. I don't think I've stopped to relax in a long time."

Linc's smile was lopsided. "Happy to be of service. Next time we race around the rink, be warned, I'm not letting you win."

The laugh bubbled out of her before she even registered it. "You sound like a sore loser, Linc." Tonight was the most fun she'd had in a long time. For once, she hadn't thought about work first. He'd even managed to tease her into a race. She still wasn't sure if he'd let her win or not, but she was going to take gloating rights where she could get them.

His smirk morphed into a mock look of shock. "How am I supposed to sound? I thought you were out of practice. How was I supposed to know I was dealing with a ringer?"

Nomi giggled. "Don't be salty. If you're good, I'll give you a rematch."

He perked up then, standing a little straighter. "You're on."

"Hell, I'll even give you a slight handicap."

His laugh was deep and rumbling and it made the hairs on her arms stand up. She liked being with him. More than she should.

"Nomi?" He took a step into her space and his voice dropped an octave.

"Yeah, Linc?"

"Since you cheated, I'm claiming my reward."

Her hackles rose, but the desperate need to feel his hands on her overrode her competitive nature with deep, pulling lust. She nervously licked her lips and met his gaze. "What do you want your reward to be?" Electric sparks danced over her skin.

"A kiss," he whispered. His moss-green eyes darkened to nearly black and she held her breath. His gaze dipped to her lips as he wound his hands around her waist.

Before she could even blink, he pressed his lips to hers. The kiss was firm and coaxing to begin, but an unseen match lit her body on fire. Nomi's lips parted on a surprise gasp and Linc took advantage. His tongue dipped in and coaxed hers into a dance as he slid over hers.

Nomi instinctively wound her arms around his neck, tentatively twining her fingers into the hair at the nape of his neck. When the pads of her fingers made contact with his skin, he growled and pressed her closer against him. Through his jeans, his erection nudged at her cleft and she arched her body into his, needing to feel more of him, needing to be closer. For once, for this moment in time, she could give in to it.

Nomi tasted so good. Sweet, with just a hint of a spicy bite. The need roiled inside him, making him shake. He'd wanted to touch her for so long, and now that he had, his senses were in overdrive. He drew back, trying desperately to pull oxygen into his lungs.

She made a tiny mewling sound in the back of her throat before her eyelids fluttered open. Her dark eyes were obsidian now, heavy with lust. Her full lips parted. Perfect for kissing.

She ducked her head and shook it slightly.

He lifted her chin so she had to meet his gaze. "What's the matter?"

"I'm not staying, Linc."

His heart pinched. But he wasn't a fool. He'd rather have her with him for a few days, then not at all. "C'mon, Nomi, take a chance."

They stood outside her door, locked in each other's gazes for seconds, minutes, hours. Finally, she raised up on their tiptoes and looped her arms around his neck. "Maybe it's time to welcome me home."

Her lips were feather light and cotton candy soft as she brushed against his. Linc let her lead the slow fusion of their lips, allowing her to be in control, despite how much he wanted to take charge. To push her to open for him. Push her to *see* him. To see how he felt about her. But he forced his body under control. Forced his mind behind the reins and not the thick, sweet, thrumming of desire.

Nomi released one hand to fumble with the door behind her. Helping her out, he dealt with the key and the lock and walked them inside, slamming the door behind them.

He pulled her against him, molding her body to his. His erection throbbing against her belly and blood rushing in his ears as he dipped his tongue into her mouth.

Nomi drew in a shuddering breath and Linc groaned, the little breathy sounds she made driving him crazy. He turned them around to brace her against the door and she moaned, tilting her hips into his body.

Skin on fire, he tore his lips from hers to kiss along her jaw. Nomi whimpered as she tried to drag him closer. When he reached the hollow of her neck, right behind her ear, he sucked gently, relishing the shiver that wracked her body.

"Linc.."

He wanted to consume her. Lust made his head swim. He needed to get his shit under control or he'd lose it.

But Nomi didn't help. She slid her hands under his coat, then tugged up his sweater. The moment her hands slid over his lower back, his skin flamed.

Linc hitched her up, planting himself more firmly between her legs, and she wrapped those long stems around his waist. The result was his cock nudging against her sweet, heated cleft. "You are so perfect."

Chapter 11

Nomi moaned. She was on fire from her toes to her thighs to her breasts to the roots of her hair; her whole body was on fire for Linc. He rocked his body into hers again and she whimpered. The way he nudged her with the steel length of him, she was already tight, too tight, ready to snap.

With an impatient snarl, he tugged her jacket free, and there was a tangle of arms and contortions to get it off. He yanked off his own more easily, all the while bracketing her against the door with his hips.

His hands stole under her Henley and he hissed as he nuzzled her neck. "So soft," he mumbled.

Nomi's head spun as she tried to make sense of what he was making her feel, but the thrumming desire in her blood eventually just took over. When he went back to kissing her, he held her face in his hands, expertly slanting his lips over hers, taking over and commanding the kiss. He slid his tongue over hers, sipping and sucking on it, until her mind fogged and all she could think about was getting closer to him. Melding their bodies and never letting go.

Nomi tugged on his sweater, and she could feel him smile into the kiss as he dragged it up. He broke their contact to release it over his head. She slid a glance over his pectorals, then his abs.

The smug smile was even in his tone as he said, "My turn." He tugged her Henley up hem first and pulled it over her head. Too weak to make her arms work properly, Nomi let him do the work. The shirt made the same soft thud his had.

Linc's eyes pinned on her breasts, watching in fascination as she breathed in a deep breath.

Never taking his gaze off her, he smoothed his hands up over her ribs. She sucked on her bottom lip as his hands drew closer to her breasts.

When Linc reached her bra, he paused and dragged his gaze to her eyes. He waited until he had her full focused attention before dragging his thumbs over the lace tracing her nipples.

Unable to look away, the tension coiling inside snapped. The fast hard orgasm spiked through her like a lighting bolt. With electric sensations lighting her up internally like a Christmas tree, she rolled her head back, breaking contact.

"No, baby, look at me. I want to see what you look like when you come."

Nomi dragged leaden eyelids up to meet his burning gaze. Even as an aftershock skipped through her body, making her weak, he watched with a focused intensity. Looking like a man ready to feast.

Sexy and low, his void tripped over her skin like a caress. "Do you have any idea how beautiful you are?"

Slowly he rolled her nipples between his thumb and forefinger through the fabric. The motion sent a spike of lust through her, straight to her core. "I could watch you respond to my touch all day."

She wanted him to do more than watch. She wanted him closer, his body over her. Inside, filling her, making her slow down and see only him.

Linc lifted her away from the door and carried her to the bedroom. He lowered her feet to the floor and kissed her leisurely, as if they had all the time in the world.

He took his time even though she could feel how hard he was, how much he wanted her. With one hand, he unfastened her bra and helped her slide her arms free.

The back of her knees hit the bed and she reached for his belt. But he stayed her with a hand. Leisurely kissing her. He removed his belt himself, and shucked his jeans off, tossing something onto the side table.

Wallet maybe? He never once broke their kiss. With his boxers still on, he eventually guided her to the bed, following her down and nestling between her thighs. He kissed her slowly, exploring the depths of her mouth. Taking his time to explore. His hands were exploratory and playful as they skimmed her body.

Now that her breasts were free, he all but ignored them. He teased and kissed the valley between, brushed his lips along the undersides of her breasts; the only contact he made with her nipples was to blow over the peaks lightly.

When she attempted to drag him closer, he lightly palmed one before wrapping his lips over the sensitive bud and licking leisurely.

"Oh yes," she moaned and clutched his head to her.

He teased with his teeth and Nomi arched her body into the caress, pulling him close. He slid his hand down her torso, over her stomach to the elastic edge of her leggings. Nomi's breath hitched and her hips rose, instinctively seeking his touch.

He took slow pulling tugs at her breast, teasing the tip. All the while, he slid his hand under the elastic. His fingers were like heat-seeking missiles. When he found her slick center, he moaned against her skin. "Fuck, you're wet."

He slid a long finger inside and she rocked her hips into him, begging for more. She needed him deeper. "More."

When he slipped another into her, she cried out. He kept a steady rhythm, sinking into her as he kissed his way down her chest. Only pausing long enough to yank her clothes down her legs.

When she lay bare before him, Linc kissed his way up her body, splaying her legs wide. With one deep stroke of his tongue, Nomi shook and clawed at the pillows behind her, afraid to let go, lest she break into a million pieces. As he traced circles around her clit, he stroked her deep with his fingers, drawing out slowly, letting her feel every inch of his strokes, making her crave more of it. Making her need it.

He loosened his lips over her hypersensitive clit and Nomi shook violently. When he sucked deep again, she broke apart in his arms. With what sounded like a grunt of satisfaction, he kissed her inner thighs, pulling himself up her body and kissing her lazily and strategically, making her blood spike again.

Nomi reached for his boxers and teased her fingertips against the elastic. Linc froze, his body going rigid. "Nomi."

She dragged down the zipper as she whispered, "Yeah."

"I—uh…" When she reached inside his boxers and palmed his throbbing erection, he stopped being coherent.

"Were you saying something, Linc?"

Against her shoulder, he shook his head. "N-no. Fuck no."

Nomi stroked the length of him, teasing the crown with her thumb, running it over the soft, smooth tip. "That's what I thought."

Gently, Nomi retreated to the base and back again. As he hissed, Linc braced his arms on either side of her head, levering his weight off her body. She circled the crown of his erection again with her thumb and one hand snapped to her wrist. "Nomi—do you have any idea how close I am right now?"

She sucked on her bottom lip as her gaze dipped to his impressive erection. "You can show me."

With a growl, he gathered both of her hands and placed them over her head. "Can you be a good girl and keep them here or will you be your usual stubborn and obstinate self?"

She giggled. "I can play nice. For now."

Laughing and shaking his head, her rolled away from her and lost the boxers. She was right about what he'd tossed on the nightstand. He dragged a condom out and sheathed himself. When he rolled back and settled between her thighs, his expression was of mock surprise. "Will wonders never cease? You listened to me."

Nomi shrugged, "It's been known to happen."

He nipped her shoulder. "Cheeky." As he placed hot, open-mouthed kisses along her neck and jawline, he teased one of her nipples to a hardened bud with his fingers. Desire spiked in her blood and she bit her lip as she angled her hips up.

On first contact, Linc cursed. She blinked up innocently. "Look, Linc, no hands."

Laughing, he sucked her bottom lip into his mouth. "*You* are a rule breaker."

"Bender. I'm a rule *bender*."

She lifted her hips again and Linc held her in place. "Nomi, I'm trying to slow down."

She shook her head. "We can go slow next time. I need you now." She emphasized her desperation with another slow roll of her hips.

"Hell." Linc dropped his forehead to hers as he pressed into her. He shifted both hands to hers, interlacing their fingers as he slid into her. Despite her need, he took his time. Sweat popped on his brow as he rocked into her. Slow slide, then even slower retreat. Deeper slide, another retreat. He played her like a violin, building her desire like a crescendo.

Patience had never been one of their virtues, so she had to break one of his rules. Freeing one hand, she wound it around his back, scoring the flesh with lightly with her nails. Linc's breath hitched, and his hips increased their tempo just a little bit.

But she wanted more. She wanted him to lose control, just like she was, wanted him to possess her. "I won't break, Linc, make love to me. Please." She punctuated it with another taste of her nails.

His answering growl was low as he scooped a hand under her ass and tucked her closer against him. Control gone, he gave her want she wanted, marking her with love bites, and dragging her up to the peak of the mountain.

Reaching between them, he found the little bundle of nerves that was the key to her pleasure. Pressing on the button gently, as he sank deep, he whispered against her lips. "Come for me, Nomi."

And she did, breaking apart in his arms as he loved her. As a starburst of bliss cascaded through her body, he tensed above her, holding her tight to him. She would have sworn, she heard him whisper, "Home."

Chapter 12

Nomi turned toward the wash of sunlight and stretched her arms over her head. Her body ached in places she'd long forgotten about. Her breasts, the deep ache between her thighs, the rug burn on her back from the middle-of-the-night session with Linc. Her knees from when she'd wrapped her mouth around the thick length of him in the shower.

Linc. She snuggled deeper in the bed. She'd really slept with Linc. And not just *slept* with him, but had sheet-clawing, body-aching sex so good, no battery operated boyfriend would ever do again. That man knew his way around her body.

She cracked an eye open to glance at the clock. Seven o'clock. That meant it was officially Christmas morning. With a groan she rolled over, only to roll into a wall of muscle.

Linc's voice was deep and raspy. "Do you know you

sleep like a crazy person? I had to wake up twice to keep you from rolling off the bed. I was worried you'd hit your head or something."

Nomi's eyes popped open and she scrambled back in bed several inches. "Linc," she gasped.

His grin was slow and sexy. "I'm glad you remember my name. I don't think I heard it enough last night." He licked his bottom lip then whispered, "Come here."

"I—uh, what are you doing here?"

He raised an eyebrow. "Well, if you let me, I'd like to taste you again."

A warm flush started in her chest, then crept over her body. "I mean, I thought you would have left."

His brows snapped down. "Did you want me to leave?

She shook her head quickly. "N-no. Of course not. I didn't know if you were staying, and after the last time, I sort of passed out."

Linc shook his head even as he pulled her to his warm body. "Nowhere else I'd rather be this morning."

She searched her brain, but all she could come up with was "Oh."

"Relax, Nomi, and let me hold you."

She didn't need to be told twice. As soon as she was encased in his strong hold, her body started to melt. "Sorry. I just didn't expect you to stay."

"I gathered."

How was she supposed to tell him that when she slept with someone the tacit agreement was that they were gone in the morning? "I hope I didn't keep you up."

His laugh was quick. "Are you kidding? After the thing you did with your tongue, I think I was in a coma."

She tucked her head and laughed into his chest. "Okay, truth be told, I *was* a little worried I'd killed you."

"And what a way to go." He kissed her forehead, then sat up. "I have something for you."

She blinked. "Oh wow, you didn't have to get me anything. Especially after you've been so nice and shuttled me around."

He pushed the covers back and stood. Nomi's mouth went dry at the sight of his strong powerful body. Linc was all lean muscle; tanned, smooth skin and powerful, but somehow graceful. Moving like a man who was comfortable in his own skin.

He rummaged in the bag he'd brought with him skating last night. When he turned around, he was semierect and it gave her a couple of sinful ideas.

His gaze turned hot when he tracked the direction of her gaze. With a smirk he said, "Keep looking at me like that and we're not getting out of bed this morning."

Right about now, not getting out of bed sounded like a fantastic idea. *Don't go getting all attached, girl, you're not staying. You have a life in Los Angeles. Do. Not. Get. Attached.* Only problem was, she liked him. And she liked how he made her feel. Slightly on edge, like anything could happen. "Who said anything about getting out of bed?"

His smile was quick as he climbed back into bed with her. "But first I want to give you this before you put another spell on me and actually do put me in a coma this time."

Nomi sat up, eyeing the small box he held in his hands. She did love presents. "You know you shouldn't have."

He eyed her chest. "How about you drop your sheet and we'll call it even?" He winked.

"You're easy, aren't you?"

"Yep."

Nomi shook her head. "You're going to have to work a little harder than that."

His grin turned wolfish. "Done." He held out the box to her.

Sitting there, bare chested, with the sheet thrown over his lap, holding out a present to her, he looked a little like how she remembered him. Boyish and silently watchful.

She accepted the box and studied it carefully. "Is shaking allowed?"

His eyes widened. "Why would you want to? Aren't you just going to rip it open?"

She made a face of mock alarm with wide eyes and forming an O with her mouth. "What? Half the fun is guessing."

The corners of his lips tipped into a smile. "Then by all means, shake. Gently."

"Too small for shoes."

He shook his head. "No. Not shoes."

She made a series of guesses, each more outrageous than the last. And he laughed along with her. Finally she just gave in and tore the paper open. When she lifted the cover of the plain pink box her breath caught. Nestled inside was a music box with a ballerina on top.

Her heart thundered, and all of a sudden there wasn't enough air. She couldn't breathe.

When she didn't say anything, instead starting at the music box, Linc filled the silence. "I hope I got it right. I remember that you used to really like them."

With shaking hands, she reached out to finger the delicate ballerina on top. "It's beautiful." She glanced up at his expectant face. "I don't know what to say. When did you get this?"

"Yesterday when you and Jilly were chatting. Did I get it right? I remember when you were kids, Jilly got you one for Christmas once. I also remember you used to dance, so I figured maybe a ballerina or something. If you don't like it, I can return it."

Nomi snatched up the ornate music box and held it to her chest. The detailing was beautiful. Something like this couldn't have come cheap. "No. I mean, it's too much, and you shouldn't have gotten something so extravagant."

He just shrugged. "I know how hard it is for you to come home. I wanted to give you something special so you'd remember it well."

Oh hell. Tears pricked her eyelids and she blinked them back rapidly. She was not going to cry. Despite herself, tears welled in her eyes. "I don't know what to say."

"Say you love it."

She grinned broadly before launching herself into his lap and wrapping her free arm around him. "I love it. Thank you. You've been great, and I know I was a bit of a pain in the ass the last couple of days and I'm sorry. I am really grateful to you." She sat back, still clutching the box to her chest. "Which is why I'm so glad I did a bit of shopping the other day for you."

His brows shot up. "When? And I didn't expect—"

She waved him off with a hand. "It's not anything big. But I asked Jilly what would be a nice way to say thank-you. She made what I hope was a good suggestion."

"Still, you didn't have to, Nomi. I was happy to help. Besides, it gave me some time to hang out with you. Which is all I really wanted anyway."

"Would you shut up and just open it? If possible, I love giving presents more than I love getting them." She pulled a box from the bedside drawer and handed to him.

Linc stared at the box for a moment, then up at her. "Thank you, Nomi."

"No, honestly, thank you. You've been great and, well, I figure I should repay your kindness for agreeing to go with me to my parents' house tonight."

"Don't forget you're already going to drinks with me at my folks' house, so this really wasn't necessary."

"Okay, fine, then look at it as a helping-me-love-Christmas-again present. I don't know. Just open it."

She bit her thumbnail nervously. Maybe she'd been too presumptuous. Maybe he wouldn't want it.

He lifted the cover of the box and his body went still. For several long moments thick silence hung in the chasm of space between them.

Unable to take it for much longer, Nomi started to ramble. "I'm sorry if it's not what you would have wanted. You said you didn't do that anymore. But I remember you being really good, so I thought maybe it was a time thing. Maybe I could remind you how much you loved it, like you reminded me last night that there are some things about being here I love. Is this okay?"

Linc held up the 50 mm camera and examined it. Silently, he removed the lens cap, adjusted the lens, then snapped a photo of her.

Oh shit. Nomi ducked. "Oh my God, Linc! What are you doing? I don't have any makeup on and I'm pretty sure I'm raccoon eyed from last night. And *hello*, naked here."

He laughed. "You look beautiful. Besides, that sheet is covering more than your dress did last night."

She pulled the sheet to herself and put out her hand to keep him from taking any more photos. "You're nuts."

He laughed. "Maybe, but I'm also extremely grateful. It's been a while since I held a camera. I guess I've been looking for a reason to love it again."

"I know it's not fancy. Hell, it's not even digital, but maybe you can play around with it a little." She shrugged. "I don't know." She was unused to feeling unsure.

He tucked a finger under her chin. "It's perfect. Thank you."

"You're welcome."

"Now are you sure you won't let me shoot some pictures of you? I'm feeling inspired."

She laughed. "Absolutely not."

"Fair enough. Then how about I thank you properly?" He gently placed the camera on the bedside table and took her box from her and did the same.

"Lincoln Porter, you look like you have something no good planned for me."

"Oh, I think you'll like it."

Nomi giggled. "You know what they say, talk is cheap."

He moved so swiftly he surprised her; before she knew what was happening, he had her on her back and had worked his way under the sheet between her thighs. He kissed her inner thighs lightly and Nomi squirmed.

He blew gently over her sex and she slid her fingers into his hair, relishing in the luxuriant feel of his hair between her fingers.

"Do you have any idea how good you taste?" To demonstrate, he lapped at her, moaning as though he was starved for her.

She clutched for purchase of the sheet even as she held his head in place and rotated her hips into his questing mouth.

Linc varied his strokes, bringing her to the edge, then drawing back, teasing, soothing, quieting the fever. When he felt the desperate tension ebbing out of her body, he ratcheted the tension back again, sliding his tongue as deep as it would go inside of her, drawing breathy, desperate cries from her.

The orgasm started in her spine and slowly rolled out, hitting every nerve, every cell, every corner of her soul.

With a growl, he splayed her wide with strong hands and wouldn't relent, applying the pressure just how she liked it. Even as she shook and her body shivered, he didn't relent. He kept licking at her, stroking her. Pulling a response from her, marking her as his. Never letting her forget what he could do to her body.

It was only after he dragged another sobbing release from her that he kissed her thighs gently, moving up her body. He tucked her limp body against his as he nuzzled her neck. "Get some rest, Nomi. You're going to need it. I have some big plans for you today."

Chapter 13

Nomi tugged on the hem of her peacoat and Linc squeezed her hand. "Relax, okay? They're your parents and they love you."

"Yeah, sure. As evidenced by the fact they they've been to see me exactly twice since I left for LA?" Not to mention her mind wasn't in it. What she wanted to be doing was tracking down a Nolan Polk private collector. They'd met with a rep from the auction committee earlier today, thanks to Linc pulling some strings. No luck. She'd even tried the investigator *Sassy* had originally sent, poring over his files, but still had gotten nowhere. "Sorry. I still have work on my mind."

"I can help you with that." He kissed her forehead. "Deep breath."

Easy for him to say; drinks at his parents' house had been easy enough. His father was having a lucid day, so he remembered her. They'd all had a great time, and

Linc had looked really happy. She slid him a glance and tried not to think about how much it would hurt to leave him behind.

It was her mother who opened the door. With her hair up in a French twist and a simple green knit sweater dress, she looked youthful. "Nomi, I'm glad you came. I—" She faltered when she saw Linc. "Oh, Lincoln." Then she looked back and forth between the pair of them, and understanding dawned.

She supposed she should have felt bad about springing Linc onto her mom like this, but honestly, she needed a buffer. "I hope it's okay I brought Linc along. We were just at his parents' for the annual Christmas fete."

Her mother recovered quickly. "Of course. Come on in. How are you, Linc?"

Her mother slipped into hostess mode easily and gave him an easy hug. She'd been in Linc's house as much as she was at home when they'd been growing up.

He hugged her back and Nomi couldn't help but feel a little sentimental. If she lived another life, this could be a normal occurrence, dinner at her parents' house with Linc. *Just for play. Do. Not. Get. Attached.*

The moment they stepped inside, the familiar smells assailed her—the smell of the burning fire in the fireplace, the slight scent of cigars if she angled toward the study.

The pristine living room of course smelled like potpourri. She hadn't been home in five years and the room looked exactly as she'd left it. When she'd been a kid, she'd made it a point to go in there to read or study just so the room got used.

Linc and her mother carried the brunt of the conversation as they made their way to the kitchen. The smells of roasting chicken and herb-crusted potatoes wafted out to greet them.

Her father grinned when he saw her and wiped his hands on a spare dishtowel after dropping the spoon into the pot. "How's my baby girl?"

Nomi blinked in confusion. She hadn't talked to them in weeks. She normally spoke to them maybe once a month. And over the past five years she'd seen them twice in LA. They'd made excuses any other time she invited them. "I've missed you, baby." Awkwardly, she returned the hug, though it probably ended up looking like a flailing seal impression. She managed to mumble an appropriate response.

When he released her, he studied her closely. "You look too thin. Don't worry about that, though. I'll make sure you fatten up before you go back." Her dad had always been the one to do the cooking.

It was only then that her father noticed Linc, and his brows snapped down. "Lincoln? What are you doing here?"

Linc didn't even seem fazed as he came to shake his hand. "Mr. Adams, good to see you again."

"I invited him, Dad. We ran into each other at the Porters' and I thought it would be nice." Okay, small fib, but it sure beat, "We're having a fling, Dad."

Her father looked unconvinced, but still he shook hands with Linc. As they all sat to dinner, topics stayed light. They peripherally talked about her job and what she was doing back in Faith. All conversations that could be had with a stranger, which in essence, she was. Linc knew more about her life now than they did.

It wasn't until Linc excused himself to take a call

from his mother that shit got real. He squeezed her knee under the table, but the moment he let go, she felt oddly adrift and alone. In the span of days a feeling she'd long been acquainted with had become uncomfortable.

Her father started first. "Sweetheart, I don't want to pry, but is it really wise to take up with the Porter boy?"

Her mother groaned. "Charles, don't start. We just got her home."

"Take up with?"

"We weren't born yesterday. I see the looks between you."

"Linc is a friend, Dad. I'll be going back to LA as soon as I do what I came to do."

Her mother frowned. "So that's it, you'll just run back and we won't see you again?"

She didn't miss the jibe. "You know where I am. I've encouraged you to visit often. You've come twice."

The muscle in her father's jaw ticked. "Isn't this how we ended up here? You picking the wrong boy and not listening to us?"

Nomi's blood simmered to life. "I picked the wrong guy once. I was a kid and naive. And because of that you punished me. You let me be humiliated. No matter what, I'm your daughter. It's your job to protect me."

"We tried that before, remember? You don't listen. You do what you want anyway."

"When are you going to stop punishing me for that, Daddy? I was a kid. I didn't know any better. But you're still my father. No matter what, you're supposed to keep fighting for me."

Her father threw down the napkin. "What do you call uprooting you from that school and moving you here? Your mother was lucky to get the job she got. I was lucky to find a teaching position in the school. And what do you do? You go and slide back into a relationship with the exact same kind of boy that got you in trouble in the first place. Repeating mistakes and patterns of the past."

Nomi shook her head. "But that's just it. Brad wasn't Jacob. Sure, he wasn't a peach, but if you'd been paying attention, you'd have seen that I learned a little bit from the previous experience. I'm not a fool, except at the end when my own parents kept me in the dark."

"And if we'd told you, you would have dug your heels in and done what you wanted."

"So you thought, 'Oh, we'll show her'? I'm sorry. I've said it a million times. But you can't punish me my whole life for a decision I made when I was fourteen. If that's the way you feel about it, then there's really no point in me being here. I don't need your approval or your love. I've made it five years without it." Nomi didn't turn back as she walked out to find Linc.

Linc drove aimlessly for thirty minutes before pulling into the drive-through of one of the only open fast-food places on Christmas day. After taking a bite of her burger, Nomi moaned and did a little dance.

"Oh God, that's good. Or maybe I'm just hungry." She shook her head. "I'm really sorry. I didn't want you to have to hear any of that."

He shrugged. He'd certainly heard worse. "It's the holiday. Lots of people are tense."

Nomi shook her head, dislodging her braids around her shoulders. "No. I knew it was likely to be a disaster, but still I dragged you along. I thought he'd be inclined to behave if you were there, but it seems that might have made it worse, if possible."

"I guess he's not a fan of mine."

"No. It has nothing to do with you at all. It's me. And his inability to see past any mistake that I've made."

"You want to tell me about the minefield we wandered into?"

Nomi blew a stray braid out of her face. She sighed before speaking. "So you know how we moved here from Alexandria?"

"Yeah, when your mom got the job with my dad."

"Yeah, well, they got in the habit of telling everyone that it was the opportunity that brought us here. When in reality it was the need to get me away from a situation in Alexandria that brought us. Mom's job was just the means."

He waited as patiently as he could for any snippet she might share with him. He felt as if he was sixteen again, waiting for a glimpse of the real her.

"So right before high school started, my class took a tour of the new high school that was built. It was on the edge of a more affluent part of town, so it was going to be pretty economically mixed. Mom was an aid for Congressman Jeffers then and Dad was a teacher at the school. On tour, I met this boy, Jacob. His dad played for the Redskins. But they lived in Alexandria. He was nearly sixteen and like cotton candy crack to a young impressionable girl. I wasn't even in high school yet and he put the press on me. He called all the time, wanted my attention, wanted to spend time with me."

Linc smiled. "Can't say I blame the guy."

She returned his smile tentatively. "Dad couldn't

stand it. He hated the kid. Swore he was trouble. Said that I was blinded."

"Let me guess. At the time you thought he was being overprotective?"

Her laugh was harsh. "Uh, yeah. Just a little. I thought he just didn't want me dating, wanted me to be a little girl forever, all the usual stuff."

"So was he right?"

She nodded slowly. "Unfortunately. Once I started school, I saw Jacob every day. I'd get out of a class and he'd be there, but not in that sweet way of just wanting to see me, but more like in the way that he wanted to make sure I didn't see anyone else."

His hands tensed on the steering wheel. But he didn't trust himself to say the right thing.

"Next thing I knew, he was suspicious of every single friend I had. He didn't want me going out. He didn't want me leaving my own house unless it was with my parents or with him."

"What did your parents do?"

"Well, Dad could see some of it coming. Apparently Jacob had this girlfriend who'd eventually left the school. Her parents complained about harassment, but because of his father's connections everything was kept quiet."

"Guys like that are dangerous, Nomi."

She sighed. "I know that now. But at the time, I thought I had it right. Can you imagine a fourteen-year-old me in love?"

Yeah, he could. And he didn't like it. "Did he hurt you?"

It was only when she shook her head that he marginally relaxed. "Never physically. But he had this way of belittling me so completely that I prayed for a kind word from him. He had me so completely under his control."

"What did your parents say?"

"They tried to talk to me. Tried to threaten to send me away to school. When they did that, Jacob threatened my father. Dad tried to have him arrested but nothing ever came of that. Finally they decided to move. Dad lost his tenure." She shrugged. "All because of me."

"I doubt they see it like that. They love you."

"You were there. Dad sees it like that. He gave up everything because I wouldn't listen. Then we move here and inside of a year, I'd gotten another pampered rich kid who thought he owned the world."

"I'm sorry, Nomi. I guess seeing me tonight set him off."

She shrugged. "Not your fault. I'm here to do a job. When it's over, I'll go back to my life. I didn't come back here to patch things up with my parents."

A fist of cold dread settled in his belly. When she was done, she would leave him behind.

Chapter 14

Nomi felt as if she was living in a dreamland. After the past few days spent with Linc and Jilly, she realized she was actually happy to be in Faith. That happy, glowy feeling evaporated, however, the moment she and Linc arrived at the country club for the wedding.

Through the ceremony, she could feel Linc's eyes on her, as if watching for any reaction to Brad. She hadn't really felt anything. Mostly boredom. If she ever got married, she'd do it differently. She wanted it to be a party with real music and not some violin quartet.

From her position on the balcony she watched Linc brave the throngs at the bar in an attempt to get her a drink. She marveled at the way he moved. Her breathing still hadn't returned to normal from their session in the limo. He had a sixth sense about how to touch her body and make her melt.

"Well, well. Look who blew back into town. I thought they'd stopped letting charity cases in. Guess not."

Nomi's stomach seized. That shrill voice could only belong to Melanie Stanfield. When Nomi opened her eyes, she came face to face with the girl who'd made her life unpleasant in high school. The good news was, Melanie wasn't going to age well.

"Melanie, I see you're still a bitch. Good to know things don't change."

Melanie narrowed her eyes and fired death-ray glares, but somehow Nomi was less bothered by her now. "What the hell are *you* doing here? I know *you* weren't invited, as this is a society wedding."

"What are you doing back in Faith? I seem to recall you telling us all the time how you were destined for greater things."

Melanie pursed her lips. "And I am. I'm just here in the middle of hell because Brad didn't have the good sense to have the wedding in DC. You're not here to try and get him back, are you? So sad, if you are."

Nomi gritted her teeth. "I'm here as a date."

"Who was dumb enough to invite you to watch the love of your life get married to someone else?"

"Linc knows that I couldn't give a shit."

Melanie paled, then darted a glace in Linc's direction, but he had his back tuned to the balcony. "You came with Linc? Porter?"

"Not that it's any of your business, but yes."

Melanie's shrill laugh filled the deafening silence of the night air. "That's fantastic. I love it. You're here with my castoff. Let me break it to you, sister. If I can't get that man to commit, there's no way in hell he's going to commit to someone like you."

The darkness of the balcony started to encroach on

her vision, and her stomach cramped as if someone had stabbed her in the gut. "Commit?"

As if sensing a weakened animal, Melanie moved in for the kill. "Oh, he didn't tell you? I mean after I helped build his career, he got cold feet. I'm the reason anyone even knows who Nolan Polk is."

No. Nomi's lungs constricted. He wouldn't have lied to her. Would he? For what? Why would he play games with her? *Breathe, mama. Just breathe. In... Out.* "If you'll excuse me, I'll just go find my date."

Even though the hot fire of betrayal had incinerated her bones and there was nothing to hold up her muscles, she made sure she held her shoulders stiff. She found him by the bar speaking to the groom and her body seized, then planted. *Fuck.*

Whatever. Big-girl panties on. "Linc, excuse me, I know you're pretty busy, but I'm going to leave."

He grinned at her when he looked up, then seemed to register what she'd said, and his brows snapped down. "Are you feeling okay?" He completely ignored Brad, who had yet to turn around.

"No, *Nolan*, I'm not okay."

Linc's eyes widened imperceptibly, then narrowed. "Nomi."

Unfortunately for her, Brad chose that moment to turn around. Immediately his gaze skimmed over her body. "Naomi, is that you?"

"Nomi," she and Linc corrected automatically.

From what seemed like a far off distance, she heard Brad's question. "What are you doing here?"

"Apparently being lied to. But I was just leaving. Good thing I know the way."

It wasn't until she entered the main courtyard, blink-

ing away that hot splash of tears, that she realized Linc
had followed her. Okay, not followed exactly, as he was
walking toward her. His breathing was slightly labored
as if he'd run to catch her. "Nomi, listen to me."

She was not jumping on this crazy train. This was
not her circus, and not her monkeys. "I have nothing
to say to you right now. If you want to speak to me, we
can do it at your agent's office in the morning."

"Shit." He ran both hands through his hair. "Nomi,
I'm sorry."

"Don't you dare call me that." She jabbed a finger
in his chest. "That name is for friends and loved ones.
You're neither of those."

That little jibe hurt Linc more than anything. "Fuck.
I know. I should have told you."

"Should have? Are you serious right now? You could
have told me a million times. You *slept* with me. At any
time you were busy licking all of your favorite places,
you could have told me. But you chose not to."

"Nomi, wait. Please listen to me."

Anger flashed in those warm chocolate depths.
"Why would I do that? You lied to me. Please explain
why I would want to hear anything you have to say."

The panic coursed through his veins. He couldn't
lose her over this. He needed her. In just a week, he was
already too close to her. She was under his skin. "I'm
sorry. I never intended to lie to you. When you called
and said you were looking for Nolan Polk you caught
me by surprise."

"Oh, really? Because that would have been a fine
time to tell me the truth."

"It's not that easy, Nomi. That part of my life is over. I

haven't been able to shoot in years. Not anything worthwhile anyway. The camera you gave me, those are the first shots I've wanted to take in ages."

"You can stop blowing smoke up my ass." She shook her head. "God, I'm such a moron. I dragged you all over town. Was that cabin even yours?"

He had nothing to hide now. She knew everything. The one thing he wanted to know was how. "Yes, the cabin is mine. I rent it so my name won't be on any of the documentation. I learned the hard way that my anonymity is paramount."

She didn't look as if she believed him or cared. "Why lie to me, Linc? You know how badly I needed to work with you. Instead, I've been chasing my tail around looking for someone who was right next to me. Do you have any idea how stupid I feel?"

Linc rubbed a hand over his face. "I'm sorry. I didn't want to lie, but then you were strutting around in full search and destroy mode and I didn't know what you wanted from me."

"Well, if you'd pull your head from your ass, you'd see that all I want to do is show your talent to the world and pay you handsomely for the privilege. I don't want anything else from you. Nothing."

He winced. He wanted a hell of a lot more from her. "I've been trying to find a way to tell you the truth since the party. I wanted you so bad, but I've been burned before."

Her dark brows softened slightly. "Melanie?"

He nodded. "She went to Carnegie, too, and we started seeing each other at the end of freshman year. She took some of my earlier photos to a gallery owner she knew, and that was the beginning of my career. I went by Nolan Polk because I don't want my name affecting my passion. I proposed my senior year. Then everything went to shit."

"Let me guess. Melanie isn't so much a gem as she is a thorny, bristly cactus."

His chest tightened as he relived his past. "She officially became my manager my senior year at CMU. Things started to go bad as soon I started selling to bigger galleries. Suddenly it was more about being seen at the right parties and with the right people than being with me. It was an ugly breakup. And because I loved her, I hadn't played close enough attention to my contract, which stated that except for charity pieces, she was due a cut of every single sale I made for three years."

Nomi's body sagged and she expelled a long breath. "That's why you stopped producing."

"My contract is officially over tomorrow. I can start selling photos again."

Nomi crossed her arms. "I see she's still bitter."

"Just a little. When you showed up wanting my work, I wasn't sure what to do with that. She taught me not to trust anyone, and you were so driven I thought you would put what you needed before how I felt."

Nomi flung her arms out. "Linc, that's not me. We could have talked through your concerns. You know how I feel about your work. The whole thing should have gone something like this. 'Hi, Nomi, long time. Which piece would you like?' I purchase. Easy. Done. Then you ask me out."

He stepped forward and reached for her, but she pulled back out of his reach. "Nomi, forgive me. I just wanted you to want me for me before you knew I was Nolan Polk."

Her voice was soft. "Why?"

Linc studied her closely. Needing to touch her. "Why what?"

"Why did you pretend to care about me? I mean, fine, it's only been a week, but you made it sound—" She stopped short.

Fuck if she didn't want to be touched; he had to make her understand. He brushed a stray tendril from her face. "Nomi, I told you the truth. I've been fascinated with you since you first showed up in Faith. And this time you were here and single and I wanted you to see me for me and not what I could do for you."

Nomi shook her head. "You only gave me part of you."

"I know." He traced his thumb over her cheek. "I should have trusted you. Please let me make it up to you tonight. Anything you want to know."

"Linc, I leave tomorrow. I don't think this is a good idea."

The tightness around his chest squeezed to a pain point. And he dragged in a ragged breath. " Let me earn your forgiveness. I know you're leaving, but give me the day."

She shook her head. "Linc—"

"Don't pull back. Not after what happened this week." He cupped her face.

"You lied to me."

"And I'm begging you to forgive me. I fucked up. I know it. Give me one more day to make it right. Stay."

He held his breath as she shifted from foot to foot. He could feel her emotionally pulling back, could feel her distancing herself, so her words surprised him. "Okay, I'll stay."

Chapter 15

This is a mistake, the tiny voice in the back of Nomi's mind whispered to her. *You'll only get hurt.* No. She would not get hurt, because this was just for now. She wasn't getting attached to him. Especially not knowing what she knew now.

The drive out to the cabin was a dark and silent one. The tension in the car was thick and charged, with uncertainty, anticipation and remorse. Linc held her hand the whole way there, occasionally squeezing as a silent apology.

He let them into the cabin and Nomi smirked. "You had fun watching me play detective, didn't you?"

"Only a little." His grin was fleeting. "Have a seat. You want coffee or something while I get some of the images out of storage?"

Nomi frowned. "We've already been all over this place; I didn't see any photos."

Linc shrugged. "There's a converted cellar. I had it renovated and made watertight. I use it as a darkroom and storage."

A flare of remorse hit her square in the chest. She could see how, after Melanie, he thought he needed to be wary of her. She'd been a little ruthless in her pursuit. "Linc, you know I wouldn't ever use you, right? I wouldn't ever exploit you."

He paused in his movement of the table to give her a soft smile. "I know you wouldn't."

Nomi shrugged. "Maybe you don't. So I'm saying it at least once."

"Nomi, I know it."

The tightness in her chest dissipated. "Good."

He pulled out several boxes of contact sheets and slid them across the floor. "Wow, that's a lot to go through."

"Well, tell me what you're interested in and I'll send you the files."

A chance to go through all of his work? *Do not go all fangirl, do not go all fangirl, do not*—too late. The giddy squeal escaped before she could call it back.

Linc blinked then a laugh bubbled out of him. "I feel like I've got a groupie."

"How nerdy is that? A photo groupie. I've got to start getting into rock stars or something."

He laughed again and the sound rolled over her, warming her from the inside. "I think I like you just the way you are. You make me feel like a rock star, so I'm going to hold on to that feeling."

They spent the next several hours poring over the photos he'd taken in the past five years. Exotic locations, familiar locations, some she preferred better than others, but the overwhelming majority she loved.

When they got to a set of photos he took in Angola, her breath caught.

Linc's voice was quiet, lulling. "This village, the women are amazing. It's made up entirely of women. They were fascinated to see a man, especially a group of white men coming to take pictures. All of their men and eligible boys have gone off to war."

Momentarily unable to speak around the emotion clogging her chest, she massaged the sore spot. "Linc, these are beautiful."

"All of them, they're really strong. They reminded me of you." He shook his head. "I mean, there I am in a far-off land, and I hadn't seen you in at least two years, and I was pretty sure you had forgotten about me, but I was thinking of you."

Wow, and what did a girl say to that? "Seriously, they're exquisite. I'd like to use these, if you don't mind."

He shook his head. "No. Not these."

"Why not?" She didn't understand.

"These women. Their stories are really personal to me. It's part of why Melanie and I went our separate ways. She wanted to put a price on them and I wouldn't go there. I'll share them with you, but I don't want these as part of the public sphere. They trusted me with their stories and I want to keep that trust."

She nodded. "I understand. Thank you for sharing them with me."

"Is there anything else you want?"

"Okay, the photos you took of the South African university students going on protest. Then I'd love the ones in India of the Bollywood girls eager to be stars. And the ones from Hong Kong, too."

"Done, they're all yours."

"Just like that?"

"Your wish is my command."

"I could get used to the sound of that." She dragged out her laptop. "Damn it, my battery is low. "

"Okay, let me send the links to the files over to you, then you can do what you need with them. I'll attach my standard photo release, too."

"Thank you. I'll send them over to my assistant. Linc, I appreciate it. It means a lot that you'd be willing to share these with me."

His voice was low. "I should have just told you. I've just been really burned before and it taught me not to trust anyone at all."

"You can trust me, Linc."

"I know that. I should have known from the beginning."

Nomi chuckled as she put herself in his shoes. "If I'd dated Melanie, I'd be gun-shy too."

"Yeah, well, I made a lot of mistakes. I'm paying for those now."

Nomi quickly sent a note to her assistant with the links to the photos Linc had sent her. Ella, please download and store these on my server. The ones marked NP123 are for the photo spread. Thanks, girl. I'll be home in a few days.

Her screen blinked at her and she groaned as she sent the message. "Looks like my batteries are gone."

"Were you able to send what you needed?"

"Yeah, thanks. You've made me a hero."

"I aim to please."

Nomi nodded. "Can I ask you something?"

He shrugged, even as he drew the curtain back to check the weather outside. "Sure."

"Why did you quit? I mean, I understand the contract situation, but you could have still been shooting. Isn't that what Prince did? Changed his name to some unrecognizable symbol to still be able to put out music?"

He shook his head. "Not the easiest question to answer." He scrubbed a hand over his face. "I know it sounds like bullshit. But I couldn't find my muse anymore. After Melanie and Dad, I felt sort of hollow inside. But then you turned up. Shook things up for me. From the moment I saw you at the train station, I wanted to photograph you. You had that lost-doe look along with this irritating persistence. I miss it. More than I thought. You made me see that."

"Linc—" The lights flickered and everything went black.

Linc cursed. "I think there are some candles around here somewhere. It's likely the storm."

Nomi shivered.

"Are you cold?"

"A little." He slung an arm around her and the electricity skipped up her spine. The need rolled through her. She was in a world of hurt if just a touch could make her feel like this.

Linc drew her close, encompassing her into his heat. He smoothed a finger under her chin and tilted her head up. "This is how I wanted our night to end." He kissed her gently, teasing the seam of her lips with his tongue.

Nomi sighed, giving him access, and he licked into her mouth, coaxing and teasing. Her insides turned to liquid fire as he deepened the kiss, making her insides melt and her muscles loosen and liquefy. In the far recesses of her mind a little niggle of a thought pricked at her. *Enjoy him for now, because soon you'll have to leave him behind.*

Linc nipped at her bottom lip, lightly sucking on it. "What's up, Nomi? I can see your wheels spinning."

"It's nothing." She shook her head to emphasize the comment.

"Then why are you frowning?" He brushed his thumb over her bottom lip. "Don't get me wrong, it's sexy. Makes me think of all kinds of things we can get up to with this mouth of yours. But I know something is bugging you."

She chose to go with honesty. "I'll just miss you, that's all."

A hint of a frown crossed his features, but as quickly as it appeared it was gone. "Why don't you show me how much?"

Chapter 16

Bright sunlight slashed across Linc's eyes, and he blinked awake. Groaning and rolling away from the offending light, he reached for Nomi, but even though her side of the bed was warm, she wasn't there.

Blinking his eyes open and sitting up, he called, "Nomi? You're ruining my wake-up call by not being in bed." Chuckling to himself, he tossed the covers back and padded into the sitting room, but no Nomi. She wasn't in the bathroom, either. It wasn't until he wandered into the kitchen that he saw her note. "Lights are back on. Ran to the bakery down the road to grab us some breakfast. Seems I need to replenish my energy. Wonder why."

She'd signed it with a heart and her name.

He couldn't help the smile tugging at his lips or the warmth blooming in his chest. *Easy does it. She's not staying. She's not yours.* No, she wasn't, but maybe she could be. Maybe they could work it out. Maybe this didn't have to be some temporary thing. *Thinking like that will only get you hurt.* And it would hurt when she got on a plane tomorrow. He'd been mentally preparing himself for it since the moment he'd seen her again. Shielding himself from the pain of watching her walk away, as he knew she would.

He glanced around the tidy cabin where he'd isolated himself, hidden away the part of him that still needed to see and explore and be free. But Nomi had brought it out in him. She'd been home for barely a blink of a moment and already he was shooting again. He itched to have his camera in his hands. Itched to capture the beauty in things. A part of him that he'd shut off to do what he thought he had to do. Maybe that had been a mistake.

He shook his head to clear the thought. Well, he wasn't going to do that anymore. And when she got back they were going to talk about what would happen with them, because he didn't feel like letting her go.

In record time, he tidied up the bedroom and grabbed a shower, letting the hot water sluice over well-used muscles. He grinned to himself as he thought of just how well he'd used them. Being with Nomi was like being with a live wire. She said the first thing that came to her mind. And completely lacked any kind of filter. She laughed with her whole body and threw herself into every single emotion. When had he become such a sap?

Problem was, merely thinking about her made his body tight. Itchy, desperate. His cock lengthened against his thigh, and as he soaped himself up, his brain conjured up images of her on her knees, sucking him deep.

Hell. He reached over to the dial and turned the water to frigid before he could get carried away. He'd rather have the real thing. Once he was dressed, he grabbed his laptop and booted it up. He scanned and discarded the usual emails. But one from his agent caught his eye. Subject: So Glad You Changed Your Mind.

When he opened it up, his stomach pitched.

Linc, I'm so glad you changed your mind about this. I got the proofs first thing this morning. And they look great. They must have worked overnight to get these up. I've always said this was your best work. I went ahead and signed the contract since you've already given the release. Call me when you get this. Since you're obviously ready to work again, I have some other opportunities to go over with you.

Linc pulled up the proofs. A little voice in the back of his skull told him not to look. But he couldn't help himself.

Instead of the photos they'd selected together, she'd used the images from Angola. The pain cut through his chest swiftly. She'd gone behind his back.

"Hi, honey, I'm home," Nomi called out, but there was no response. She dropped the bag of bakery goodness on the kitchen table. "Linc, are you here?"

After a quick check of the bedroom and the cellar, she realized he wasn't anywhere in the cabin. But it wasn't until she checked the living room that she saw his note stuck with a Post-it on his laptop. "I thought we had a deal. Took a cab back. Leave the car at Jilly's when you're done."

Her stomach cramped. He'd left her. Abandoned her. She forced herself to take several deep breaths while her rational brain took over. She pulled out her packing boxes and tried to file away the pain of being ditched.

She snatched the Post-it off the laptop and crumpled it. The motion activated the laptop screen and bile rose in her throat. "Oh God." *Ohgodohgodohgod.* "No, no, no." The image of the woman from Angola stared back at her with her hauntingly beautiful eyes. Under the heading of *Sassy* magazine.

Her brain finally came online and she sprang into action. This had to be a mistake. It was a mistake. She hadn't approved those photos. She'd sent them to Ella to put on the server and told her which ones to use. This wasn't supposed to happen.

When rummaging in her purse didn't produce the results she wanted, she tossed the entire contents on the kitchen table sending lipstick and keys and wallet and bobby pins flying. She snatched up her phone and dialed quickly. Belinda answered on the first ring.

"Nomi, I must say, when you say you're going to deliver, you're not kidding."

"Belinda, we need to pull those photos. Those aren't the ones we're meant to use."

"What do you mean, pull them? The mocks have already been sent and approved. The issue is supposed to ship in a week. I'm not pulling the images. What's wrong with you? You do realize that the whole point of you going into the belly of the beast, as you put it, was to get these images?"

Nomi massaged her temples. "Yes, I know, but the wrong images were used. I'm due back tonight. I was going to select a few different options. That picture was not for all eyes. It was for my eyes only. I gave my word."

"Sorry, Nomi, if you didn't want the photos up for option, then you shouldn't have put them on the server."

On the public server? "What? I didn't. I sent them to Ella for my *personal* server. She wouldn't."

"I don't know what to tell you," Belinda said. "Amber pulled the images and selected them herself. She even gave you full credit for delivering on Polk."

That bitch. "Look, I don't know what happened, but she should never have had access. We are not working together on this."

"Don't worry about it." Belinda said, as if she understood. "I know she's doing the whole riding-on-your-coattails thing and wants to peripherally have credit. I know you're the reason we can even do this issue."

How the hell had everything gotten so screwed up? "Shit, Belinda, yes, I want the credit, but what I really care about is the promise I made to the photographer. I gave my word that I wouldn't use those images."

"I'm sorry. We're going with these."

Damn it. She needed to find Linc. She needed to make him understand. Make him see. She wouldn't have done this to him. She cared too much about him.

Chapter 17

With little regard to the snow and the sheets of ice, Nomi drove like mad to Jilly's place. Twice she almost spun out. Once she almost rear-ended another driver. And more than once she fishtailed. But she finally made it to Jilly's place in one piece. Too bad she bought it and fell on her ass the moment she stepped out of the car.

"Damn it to hell."

Jilly came out of the gallery, half laughing. "Shit, Nomi, are you okay?" But she couldn't mask the humor under the worry.

Nomi dusted off her legs as she attempted to get her knees back under her. "Laugh all you want. I'm actually here for Lincoln. Have you seen him?"

Jilly pursed her lips. "Nomi, I'm sorry. He came through about an hour ago. He's pretty pissed."

"I know. And it's a total mistake. I never would have betrayed him like that. I know what those images meant to him. It was totally a mistake. I never would have done that. I'm trying to fix it right now. Do you think I might be able to see him?"

Jilly sighed as she shook her head. "I take it that you know who he is."

"Yeah, I had that little revelation last night. Thanks for the heads-up."

Her friend winced. "Yeah, I'm sorry about that. He's my brother, and I know what he needed was some time to figure his shit out. I hope you can understand."

"Yeah, I get it." Nomi shook her head. "I'm not even mad about it. All I want right now is to fix this with him. Is there any place he goes when he's really upset? Anywhere I'm likely to find him?"

"You've obviously already been to the cabin. Sometimes he heads to the lake."

"I passed the lake on my way back. Please think, Jilly. I don't want to go back with him thinking that I did this to him on purpose—that I would use him."

"Have you tried calling him?"

"What do you think?" Nomi pursed her lips.

Jilly tucked her hair behind her ears. "Okay, obviously, you've thought of the obvious places. Maybe there is one more. Can you drive?"

"Yes." She gingerly reached for the door, wary of falling again. "Get in."

They drove out of town about ten miles to a small farmhouse. Jilly pointed. "This was the house we lived in when we were really little. Mom and Dad kept the place."

"I don't remember ever coming out here."

Her friend shrugged. "Yeah well, there's nothing to do out here, especially for teenagers who weren't necessarily driving yet—it wasn't exactly a hangout spot. But in this case, it works. Especially if you're looking for solitude. You can pretty much see everything from this spot. With us so close to DC at night, you can get a decent view."

Nomi let Jilly lead the way into the house. There was a truck parked in the garage, and Jilly suggested he'd taken a cab to her place, then driven to the farmhouse with the truck.

Linc wasn't happy to see them at all. Despite his anger, his glare for her was hot and charged. With Jilly, it was completely different. "You couldn't keep your mouth shut, could you, Jilly?"

"Sorry, Linc, I'm a sucker for love."

Heat suffused Nomi's face. "Jilly, can you give Linc and me a minute?"

"Uh, sure thing. I'm just going to go inside and make some coffee."

When her best friend was gone, she was left with Linc.

"I'm so sorry."

He shook his head. "Not your fault, right?"

"It was. I wouldn't do that."

His brows snapped down, morphing his handsome face into a pale comparison. "But still somehow you did. I should have known better than to trust you. But I was so caught up in you."

"Linc, listen to me. The last week or so I've been home—"

He crossed his arms. "You want me to believe that you felt something? That you feel something? Been here, done this already. I don't believe you. You said it at the beginning—you were here to do a job. Nothing more, nothing less."

She shivered in her coat, and drew the peacoat closer against her body. "No, Linc. This was all a horrible mistake. There was a mix-up in communication with my assistant. Those photos should never have been published. And, look, you're right, I had one goal when I got here. It was all I could think about. I was only concerned with my job. That's what I thought I was here for, but somewhere between you picking me up and taking me around and exploring the cabin and dragging me to that wedding and going to dinner with me at my parents and ice-skating, I fell in love. I've kept myself apart from everything and you've forced me to open up and care about something again. You taught me to love this holiday again. It fills me with home and happiness to think about mistletoe now."

"Pretty words, Nomi, but then again, you're a writer. I would expect nothing less."

"Linc, please."

He shook his head. "You said it yourself. It's not like this thing was supposed to last anyway. Only temporary, right?"

That last jab sliced through her. Tears prickled behind her eyes and she blinked them away rapidly. She would not cry. She would not cry. So what if she cared about him. So what if she'd started to care about somebody. *It's not like he was special.* She'd replace him when she got back to LA. Didn't matter if the sex was so good she'd never need chocolate again. He was totally replaceable. She didn't care. "Fine. But you know the truth of who I am. You said it yourself. Listen to that truth. I'm going back to LA in the morning. You know where to find me if you want to talk it out."

"I won't be finding you to talk about anything."

She shoved her hands into her pockets and started back to the car. "I know." As she walked back to the car, she refused to turn back and look at him. There was no way she was going to let him see her cry.

"You're an idiot, you know that?"

Linc rubbed the back of his neck. "Damn, Jilly, not now, okay? I'm not in the fucking mood."

"Well, it's about time somebody told you to your face: you're an ass. A dick-headed moron who just let the woman he loves walk away over some stupid shit because he's afraid of getting hurt."

He couldn't help it; his lips twitched. "Dick-headed moron?"

"Yes." She huffed as she jabbed him in the chest. "You've been pining after that woman since we were kids. I swear, if you weren't my twin brother, I'd freaking kill you."

"Jilly, you wouldn't understand."

"What? I wouldn't understand getting hurt? Have you forgotten that my fiancé left me at the altar?"

He winced. "Jilly—"

"I know you wanted to kick his ass as much as I did. It sucked the big one. But this is different. You're hiding."

His temper flared to life. "That's enough, Jilly." They weren't going to talk about this.

"No, it is not enough. Nobody ever challenges you." She pointed into the now empty driveway. "But that woman, she challenges you. God, I remember when we were kids and she came around, I saw this version of you we'd never see unless it was just you and me together. Nomi had a way of drawing you out of your room, making you interact."

"Shut it."

"I remember that shy, withdrawn kid. The one who used to take these gorgeous candid photos of me and my best friend. I remember you trying to take care of her and making sure Brad stayed on his shit to treat her right." She inhaled deeply. "You think I don't know that you were the reason Brad was on time to that homecoming dance, because you offered to drive? You made sure he got there, even though he was already wasted."

Enough. He didn't want to think about the loser he'd been. "Enough, Jilly."

"No, not enough. You've loved her forever. Don't you think it's time you stopped being afraid and go after what you want? Yes, you got hurt, but enough hiding. Enough using Dad as an excuse not to go live your life. Grab the devil by the balls and give him a whirl."

Despite himself, the laugh bubbled up inside him. "Jesus, Jilly, that mouth of yours."

She grinned prettily. "It's why you love me." She tugged her jacket down and studied him. "Now, are you going to go after the woman you love or what?"

"It's not that easy." She didn't understand. He didn't want to believe in someone again to have her not be what he thought.

"Well, you have to trust somebody sometime, and Nomi cares about you."

"What she cares about is her job."

"She's driven and she made a great life for herself after she left. You can't fault her for it."

"And I don't." *Liar.* "But she'll always choose her job."

Jilly shook her head. "And you will always be afraid to take that step. You'll be the one missing out. At least she isn't afraid to be bold."

Jilly stalked out into the morning air and as he watched her, Linc wondered just how right she was.

Chapter 18

Nomi tapped her foot impatiently as she waited for her train. All she wanted was to take the train to the airport and get the hell out of Faith, Virginia. In the past week, she'd fallen in love, had her parents dig up and pour salt into old wounds and then had her heart broken. She'd gotten what she needed for her job, but it hardly seemed worth it.

Linc would never forgive her. He would certainly never trust her again. She'd done exactly what Melanie had done to him.

He'd thought she was just in it with him for the photos, and the end result had been what he expected, even if the intention wasn't there.

Nomi brushed her braids out of her face and secured them at the nape of her neck with a clip. She just needed to wipe this whole week from existence. She'd go back to her normal life. Work, home, work, home, the occasional date. All very surface. The way she preferred it. She wouldn't feel this kind of pain again. Because right about now, it felt like someone was pointing a blowtorch at her heart. And she wouldn't recommend it as one of her top five feelings of all time.

All she had to do was forget all about Linc. The way he looked at her. The way he tasted. The way he touched her, as if she was precious. *Stop. He isn't coming for you. There will be no grand gestures.* This wasn't a romantic comedy. This wasn't love. She could only count on herself for her happiness. Even entertaining Linc as a possibility had been a mistake. One she'd be paying for for a long time.

And this time, she meant it. She was never coming back to Faith, Virginia. The personal cost just wasn't worth it.

Her gaze flickered to the signboard as she willed time to pass faster, but unluckily for her, only three minutes had passed since she'd looked the last time.

An image in her peripheral vision made her think she was seeing things. But no. It was her father with his slightly loping gate. He wore his favorite jeans and a sweater worthy of Bill Cosby in the Huxtable days, with a leather Members Only jacket, looking like a throwback to the nineties. Nomi stood. "Dad? Is everything okay?" There was no way he was here unless something was terribly wrong.

When he reached her, his lips were set in a grim line. "Nothing's wrong, Nomi."

"Don't lie, Dad. You wouldn't be here unless there was."

He scrubbed a hand over his face. "I promise, Naomi."

This time, she couldn't help herself and she corrected him. "Nomi, Dad, I go by Nomi."

The flicker of his lips into a slight smile surprised her. "We used to call you that when you were a baby. Somehow, as you grew, we lost it."

How bad was it that she didn't know what to say to her own father. She shifted on her feet. "What's up, Dad? My train leaves in a little bit."

"You didn't say goodbye."

Really? He wanted to criticize her? "Yeah, well, you didn't exactly make it so I'd want to."

When he winced, she wished she'd held her tongue.

"Nomi, I wanted to apologize for Christmas night."

She blinked at him. "Come again?"

He rolled his shoulders back and made it a point to meet her gaze. "I was wrong. And instead of holding you and telling you how much I missed you, I pushed you away…again."

She opened her mouth then closed it. Tried again and failed. It wasn't until her third attempt that she managed words. "I don't know what to say."

His quick grin transformed his whole face, making him handsome and far less austere. "I should never have blamed you for what happened with that Jacob boy. It wasn't your fault."

Her hands shook. "I don't understand."

"You've always had this spirit. You follow your heart and have your own path. Sometimes it gets you into trouble, and as your dad, I should have been there for you emotionally to help you through. Instead, I was angry and resentful that you didn't listen. I wanted to stifle that carefree, independent voice you had."

In the distance, the train to Dulles International announced their boarding. "Dad, that's my train."

He nodded. "I won't keep you. I just saw you with the Porter boy and I lost it. I had planned on pretending the past didn't happen, to get us back on track, but then you came with him and I thought you were in the old pattern again. I should have warned you about the Lennox boy. I should have chosen to talk to you about DeWayne. Treated you like an adult. I realize that the freedom and bravery you exhibit is something I've always wished I could do myself and I didn't have the guts. I lost five years with my daughter because I couldn't admit it. I'm sorry."

Tears pricked her lids and she sniffled. As if she'd been doing it for years, she walked right into her father's arms and let him hold her. This was what she'd been missing. Family. A sense of home. She hadn't known it until she'd been forced to come back. She didn't want to be alone. It wasn't better this way. "Daddy, I have to go."

He smoothed a hand down her hair. "I know. But your mom and I, we're going to come to California for Valentine's Day. Take a second honeymoon. See our daughter."

Nomi swiped at the tears with the back of her hand. "I'd like that."

He walked her to her platform and helped her with her carry-on. "Just remember, Nomi, we love you."

Uncaring about the free flowing tears, Nomi took her seat and waved to her father as the train pulled out of the station. If nothing else, she'd found her family again. Now if only she wasn't nursing a broken heart.

Chapter 19

"Congratulations, Nomi. This is a huge coup." Belinda grinned.

Then why did she feel ill? Nomi held up the magazine and fingered the image on the front. It was a beautiful shot. She just wished it hadn't cost her the one person she'd cared about in years. Just like every other time a wayward Linc thought intruded into her brain, she bitch-slapped her inner sap. Thinking about him would only distract her.

"It's beautiful. I'm really proud of it. I just wish we'd gotten it another way. One of the others would have been great, too. I just want to forget about the whole week. In all, it turned out well, and it wasn't as bad as I thought." Especially the parts with Linc. She involuntarily winced as pain sliced through her heart.

Belinda smirked. "So the devil no longer lives in Faith, Virginia?"

Nomi smirked. "Oh, he still lives there, but he doesn't bother me anymore. I was holding on to some shit, and once I let it go, I started to have some fun."

"Fun? Will wonders never cease?"

"It's no big deal."

Belinda's laugh was clear. "Oh, really? Aren't you the same person who offered me her shoe collection to get out of going?"

"That might have been me. But clearly I was kidding. I love my Jimmy Choo shoes too much."

Belinda snorted. "Yeah okay. But the only thing that causes an about-face like this is usually love."

Nomi's heart squeezed. Yeah, love. She didn't know anything about that. *Yeah you do.* No. She didn't. Except, she missed him. They'd only had a few days together, but she missed him.

She missed cuddling in front of the fire with him and talking. When he'd made her hot chocolate and taken care of her after she'd bruised her damn tailbone. He was sweet. And the way he'd told her that she'd been all he thought about when they were kids. Why the hell had she never seen that?

If she'd known or seen him, well, things might have been different. She would have stayed. And maybe wouldn't be sitting here now.

Belinda studied her intently. "So there *is* a guy?"

"Huh? What? Don't be ridiculous," Nomi sputtered.

Her friend leaned forward. "Is it the photographer?"

Hell, how did she answer this? "It's an old friend. Things got a little complicated."

"Nothing like a little holiday distraction to chase away the blues."

"Yeah, I guess." And that was all it was. *You're the*

idiot who got attached. Only to find out that he didn't trust her, and placed her in the same category as Melanie.

"Uh oh, did you go and catch a case of feelings?"

She shook her head. "Even if I did, he didn't. So, that's all that matters."

"What if he said he'd been a total dick-headed moron?"

She whirled to find Linc lounging in the doorway to her office.

"Thanks, Belinda, I appreciate it," he said.

Nomi turned to find her boss grinning and shrugging. "What can I say? I'm a sucker for love. I'll go ahead and leave you two alone."

Once Belinda departed, she was left alone with Linc in her office. His eyes went to the magazine on the desk immediately, and she wanted to be ill. But hell if she was going to apologize to him again. "What do you want, Linc?"

He sighed. "I knew this wasn't going to be easy. It seems I keep screwing up with you."

She crossed her arms over her chest and Linc's gaze hovered in the direction of her breasts for the breadth of a second. *That's right buddy, look at them and weep.* "You made it clear that you didn't trust me or believe in me. You lie to me, I forgive you. There's a misunderstanding and you refuse to trust in me. You thought I was capable of hurting you."

"It was easier to push you away than accept that I love you."

Her breath caught in her chest, strangling her. "What?"

He leveled a gaze on her. "I said I love you."

"That's nuts." She shook her head.

"You are obstinate and determined and kind and vulnerable and fun, and that mouth of yours—you drive me crazy. I was an idiot to not trust you. I've been a little in love with you since you rolled into town, kicking ass and taking names. I knew you were unstoppable when you took your life into your own hands at seventeen and followed your dream. I don't deserve you. Please forgive me. I'm begging you for a second chance."

"Linc…"

He pulled her into his arms. "Shit, a third chance. I'm a little slow on the uptake, but I get it now. I'm never letting you walk out of my life again. I love you. I *need* you in my life."

"My life is here. Can you handle that?"

"Funniest thing. I'm a photographer, so apparently I can work from anywhere. And I want to be with you."

Relief washed through her. "I'm not very good at relationships, you know."

He smirked. "Don't worry, we'll fumble around in the dark together. As long as we have some mistletoe, we'll be okay."

"I'm serious, Linc. This love thing is foreign, and I'll screw up."

He grinned. "Love thing, huh?"

Nomi met his gaze directly. "Yes. I love you, Lincoln Porter."

"Good. It'll make living with me a whole lot easier."

* * * * *

I'd like to dedicate this story to my mother, Mary, and sister Kelsey for assisting in my brainstorming process. I could not have written this story without each of you.

Dear Reader,

I once heard a speaker at a conference say, "In the end we only regret the chances we didn't take." Well, this rings true for Sage and Grayson.

I came up with this story line after witnessing a couple in a coffee shop discussing how long it had been since they had last seen each other. I could feel their chemistry and was instantly intrigued by their relationship. Although they didn't stay long enough for me to hear their entire conversation, I was inspired. I've wanted to write a missed opportunity love story for a while and Sage and Grayson were the perfect couple.

Writing this story was also a bonding moment for my mother, sister and me. Over cheese, grapes and wine, they helped breathe life into the characters. I hope you enjoy Sage and Grayson just as much as we do.

Much love,

Sherelle Green
authorsherellegreen@gmail.com

Acknowledgments

To the lovely couple from the coffee shop…
wherever you are!

WHITE HOT HOLIDAY

Sherelle Green

Chapter 1

"If you want that beard to continue to look as white as the snow, I suggest you take two steps back." Sage Langley dangled her caramel macchiato in front of the man dressed like Santa Claus and quirked one eyebrow.

Santa lifted his plush red velvet hat and peered at her though small circular glasses. "All I did was ask you to donate money this holiday season. You walk into this store almost every day, and you never give a dime."

Sage let out a loud breath. "Listen, I already told you that I would donate money after Christmas to several charities. I don't need you harassing me every day by ringing that bell in my ear to try to change my mind."

"You're a real Scrooge," the Santa lookalike said as he went back to stand in his place on the sidewalk. "It's the most wonderful time of the year, and your attitude is anything but jolly."

She rolled her eyes as she walked past Santa. "Christmas isn't holly or jolly, and quite frankly, I dislike the day after Thanksgiving because it means I have to deal with men like you, who will spend all day dressed up in bright red suits pretending to be something they aren't. Even if Santa did exist, I'm sure he would curse the fact that we assume he has no fashion sense."

Sage was so annoyed that she didn't notice the young boy standing nearby looking at his mom with tears in his eyes.

"Santa isn't real, Momma?" Expectant eyes glanced upward at his mom.

"Of course he is, sweetie. This woman is just upset because she's worried she will get coal in her stocking."

The boy turned watery eyes to Sage. "Is that true, lady?"

Not the sad puppy dog eyes. She might not like Christmas, but she didn't have a heart made of rock. "Your mom is right—I'm just worried I will get coal in my stocking. But Santa over here assured me that if I'm good from now until Christmas, maybe I will get what I want." Sage didn't have to look at the man in the Santa suit to see the smug grin on his face.

"Then you should start being good now," the little boy told her before he ran over and hugged her legs. "For my gift, I'll ask Santa to give you what you want for Christmas."

Her heart broke, and even after the little boy left with his mom, she still stood in the same spot. She remembered a time when she felt like the young boy. A time when she'd snuck into the living room to shake her presents under the tree. Years ago, when Christmas had been her favorite holiday.

"I suspect you weren't always a Grinch," Santa said,

jarring her from her thoughts. Instead of replying, she reached into her clutch, pulled out a couple dollars and placed the money in the bright red bucket.

"Still harassing Santa?" Sage turned at the sound of her best friend's voice.

"More like Santa was harassing me."

Piper St. Patrick eyed her suspiciously. "I find that hard to believe, considering he's the third Santa I've had in the past couple weeks. You ran off the other two with your Scrooge-like view of Christmas."

Sage brushed off Piper's words as she sat in a plush vintage chair next to the checkout counter. Growing up, St. Patrick's Antiques had always been Sage's escape from small-town gossip. It was bad enough that she had been teased at school, but even worse was having the entire town of Summerland, Michigan, gossiping about the Langleys.

Which was why Sage had been itching to go to college. Then she took it one step further and taught overseas for eight years, enjoying the fact that no one knew about her father's wrongdoings in other countries.

She was grateful that her relationship with Piper hadn't changed much due to distance. Even so, it was nice to finally be in the same state as her best friend and to have landed a job at a university three hours away from the Michigan small town.

"Is your mom still surprised you came home?" Piper asked as she wiped the glass counter that displayed beautiful antique jewelry.

"She's still surprised, and of course she coaxed my brothers into taking up all my free time when I'm not here with you, to make sure I don't leave town without saying goodbye." Sage had been teaching in Ohio for a year upon returning to the United States, but had managed to land an English professor position in Michigan.

"I told my mom that I'm leaving in a couple days, though."

Piper stopped wiping the glass and glanced over at Sage with surprise. "You're leaving this week? I thought you would stay in town until after Christmas."

"I never said that. When I got here, I said I would stay in Summerland for part of my holiday break. I never said I would be here for Christmas."

Piper gave her a look of disbelief. In all honesty, she'd originally had every intention of staying for Christmas. However, she had underestimated the memories that would come flooding back the longer she was in town.

"Look, Piper," Sage said as she rose from the chair. "I promise that I will come home more often, but I really don't think I can be here Christmas Day." If there was one person who knew exactly how she felt, it was Piper.

"I think you've been running too long." Piper walked around the counter to stand next to Sage. "Sometime, you'll have to face your past and learn to move forward."

Before Sage could respond, the door of the store chimed.

"Hello, ladies."

Both women turned just as Sage's brother Tate Langley, approached them.

"Hey, Tate," Sage said, although she wasn't really sure he'd heard her. His eyes were glued to Piper just as hers were glued to him. When they were in high school, she'd always known Piper had had a crush on her brother, and from what she remembered, her brother had had a crush on Piper, too. But for some reason, they'd never dated.

Sage had never told her brother not to date her best friend or vice versa. She wouldn't dare, considering she'd also had a crush on her brother's best friend growing up. When Sage had been overseas four years ago, she had received a call from Piper telling her she was getting married. She'd asked her about her feelings for Tate, but Piper had dodged the question. Observing the two now, she wished she'd pushed Piper a little more for an answer.

"How's Jeremy?" Tate asked, his eyes still fixed on Piper. Since Sage had been home, Jeremy had been out of town twice already. If she hadn't been maid of honor at their wedding, she wasn't sure if she'd even believe they were actually together.

"He's fine. Working, as usual."

Tate stepped a little closer to Piper. "Hmm. Doesn't he know he shouldn't leave a wife as beautiful as you all alone for too long?"

"Stop it," Piper said as she lightly punched Tate in the arm. It wasn't unusual for her brother to be flirting with Piper even though he had a serious girlfriend. Nor was it unusual for Piper to flirt back. But Sage sensed there was something deeper there that she couldn't quite put her finger on. She knew that neither Piper nor Tate would ever cheat on their significant others, but the air around them was different now than it had been during her last visit, and she suspected neither of them were happy in their current relationships.

"Tate, did you need something?"

Tate finally turned away from Piper to look at Sage.

"Actually, I saw you outside the store window and was happy to see you hadn't left town."

Sage sighed. "Am I that predictable?"

"Yes, you are. Which is why I'm here to offer you another escape besides spending Christmas all alone in your townhome."

"I wouldn't be alone." She extended both hands. "I'll have Merlot and Chardonnay to keep me company."

"Oh, in that case, I guess you don't want to know how Grayson and I can help you."

Her body quivered slightly at the mention of Grayson's name. Except for the conversation she'd had with him at Piper's wedding, she hadn't seen Grayson in years. Not only did she lose her cool every time she was around him, but since he was her brother's best friend, she knew having him in her life was inevitable, which annoyed her way more than she wished it did.

"How can you help me?"

Tate pulled out a key ring with three keys on it. "By handing you these."

Sage took the keys and looked at Tate questioningly. "How exactly will a set of keys help me?"

Tate raised an eyebrow. "You don't remember?"

"Remember what?"

"Check out the words on the key chain."

She squinted as she read the words etched in red. "Oh, my gosh," she squealed. "You're giving me the keys to your vacation home in Punta Cana?"

Tate chuckled at her eagerness. "Technically, it's Grayson's vacation home, since my home is under renovation. But as you know, our homes are right next to one another. Interested?"

"Of course I am! But wait, weren't you supposed to be going there with Olivia?"

Tate stole a glance at Piper before answering. "Yeah, but we decided not to go. We were going to leave tomorrow and be back the day before Christmas, but something came up. I talked to Grayson, and he's okay with you going in my place and staying after Christmas if that's what you want."

There's that name again. "Will Grayson be in the Dominican Republic, too?"

Tate's face grew serious. "He better not be there when you're there. He assured me he'd be visiting his brother in Miami and spending Christmas there."

"Oh, okay. I was just making sure, since I want the place all to myself."

"Yeah, right," Piper mumbled before Sage had a chance to nudge her. *Goodness.* She was thirty-two years old, and her brother still treated her like a child. She wanted to tell him to save his frustration because Grayson Ellington had made it clear years ago that he wasn't interested in her romantically, so big brother had nothing to worry about.

"You always were my favorite brother." She stood on tiptoes to give him a hug. "I will definitely accept the offer to go to Punta Cana."

Tate shook his head with a laugh, since she'd just told their younger brother, Isaac, that he was her favorite when he told her he'd made her favorite dish yesterday for the family dinner.

"Just make sure you see Mom and Isaac before you leave."

"I will."

For a day that had begun on a rather sour note, it

was definitely turning positive now. Beaches, islanders, relaxation and a vacation home all to herself. Christmas was ten days away, and there was no doubt in her mind that this would be her best non-Christmas celebration yet.

Chapter 2

Grayson Ellington glanced at his watch as he hopped into his rental car and blasted the air. Any other time, he'd love to have the windows down to cool off, but today, he was experiencing a new type of heat.

Ever since he'd received a call from his best friend, Tate, he hadn't been able to think about anything else but Sage Langley. It wasn't really unusual for her to be on his mind, but knowing that he had a chance to be alone with her and explore a suspicion that he hoped like hell was true was enough to make him drive slightly faster than normal.

He glanced out the window at a man and woman on the back of a motorbike lugging three armfuls of groceries. That was one of the things he loved about the Dominican Republic. The natives were some of the most hardworking people he'd ever met.

As the gates that offered seclusion for several vacation homes that sat on a private beach came into view, his mind drifted to Sage again. According to Tate, she'd arrived earlier in the morning. He gave a quick nod to the security officer and flashed the pass needed to enter the gate.

Once he'd entered the premises, he drove down the long, narrow road that was encased by palm trees. He turned off the air so that he could let the breeze seep through the windows. He hadn't been to his Punta Cana vacation home in almost two years due to his demanding career as attorney general. Now that he had a chance to soak in the island he loved like a second home, he made a silent promise to never let that much time pass again.

Grayson and Tate had visited the Dominican Republic for the first time when they were both in grad school. Back then, Punta Cana didn't have nearly as many tourists and resorts as it did now. They'd only had the property for a couple years before others began buying and building homes. They decided to each build a vacation home next to one another, but with enough distance between them to offer seclusion. At the time, they were just starting their careers, and the logical solution seemed to be to combine incomes and build one massive home. But the more they'd thought about it, the more they had realized they may need more privacy if they ever had decided to vacation at the same time. Staring at his three-level beachfront home over a thousand feet away from Tate's, he really appreciated the fact that they'd chosen to have separate homes. Especially if that meant Sage Langley would be occupying his place.

"Almost 6:00 p.m.," he said to himself as he pulled

into the driveway. Her rental car was there, so he knew she had to be inside. He thought once more about the cover story he was going to give Sage so she wouldn't expect he was here under false pretenses.

He pulled down his visor and looked into the mirror. "Okay, I'm here for a business meeting for one of my top clients who is here on vacation. I should only be here for a few days, and I can stay in the basement or on the second floor. Your choice. I actually forgot you were here until I was already on the plane."

He shook his head. "No, scratch that last line. There is no way Sage will ever buy it." She knew him too well to believe he could ever forget that she was in the Dominican Republic until he was on the plane.

"My client is currently here in the DR, and he had an urgent matter that needed my immediate attention." He squinted his eyes in the mirror as he observed his facial expressions.

"Hmm, maybe I should smile when I say it rather than try to keep a straight face."

He was two seconds away from practicing faces in the mirror before he caught himself and let out a hearty laugh. "I'm a grown-ass man talking to myself in the mirror before approaching a woman I've known almost my entire life." He leaned his head back in the seat.

His cover story wasn't a complete lie. He really did have a client who was here with his family, and they had a home in the same area about a half mile down the road. And he really did plan on meeting with the Henderson family while he was here. But he didn't have to travel thousands of miles for a conversation that could take place in the United States. There was only one person he would go to such great lengths to get alone, and he doubted she had any idea what plans he had in store for her stay in Punta Cana.

When he first began developing more than friendly feelings for Sage, he was fine with compressing those feelings until they went away. After years of trying to convince himself that he didn't feel strongly about her, he'd finally concluded that his feelings wouldn't go away unless he did something about them.

With all the confidence he showed in court, he got out of the car and made his way to the door. After a few knocks and a minute of waiting, she still hadn't come to the door.

"Crap," he said, knocking once more. *I really don't want to use my keys.* Not only was he afraid that walking into the home, despite the fact that it was his, would scare her, but he also didn't want to seem intrusive. He didn't know anyone who disliked Christmas as much as Sage, and even though he planned on changing her view of the holiday while he was here, Tate had confirmed that years of being overseas hadn't changed the sour mood she had all through December.

After he tried knocking for a third time, he finally decided to use his key. He took precaution as the door opened and called out to Sage several times before closing the door and taking a look around.

"Where is she?" The sun had set, and he doubted she'd be walking around at night when she didn't know the area too well. The central air was on, and some sort of pasta dish was sitting on the stove, so she had to be nearby.

He'd just made it to the second floor when he heard the sound of running water and a sultry voice floating from the bathroom down the hall. *Why isn't she show-*

ering in the master suite? He leaned on the wall and listened to a sound he hadn't heard in years. That voice, that soft yet husky voice, had gotten him over a lot of hard days when they were younger. It wasn't that Sage could sing. In all honesty, she could barely hold a tune.

It was the vibrations in her voice that always got him hooked. He'd bet she would have been a great spoken-word poet, if she were into that sort of thing. Trying to ignore the sultriness in her voice was one of many things he constantly had to remind himself to do.

He'd moved to Summerland, Michigan, during eighth grade, and he'd quickly made friends with Sage's brother Tate. Grayson had immediately put Sage in the little sister category, and it helped that even when she got to high school and he was about to graduate, she remained his best friend's scrawny little sister.

But he could still remember the first time he had to run home and take a cold shower after being around Sage all day. Sage and her friend Piper had begged him and Tate to take them along on their fishing trip. Of course, Tate didn't want them to go, but after some persuading by the girls, they both eventually agreed to let them tag along. Biggest mistake ever.

Grayson could have dealt with the fact that the boat was so small, sixteen-year-old Sage couldn't help but brush up against him. He also could have handled the crazy rainstorm that had come out of nowhere and almost capsized their boat. What he hadn't been able to deal with was waiting out the storm huddled together under a bridge while Tate and Piper went to get the car that was parked on the other side of the lake. To this day, he had no idea how that arrangement had happened, and even worse, while he should have been making sure his best friend's little sister was warm, he spent the enter time getting very familiar with each curve of her body. Curves that he could have sworn had never been there before.

For a hot-blooded college freshman, he hadn't been able to control his curiosity, especially when Sage made no attempt to stop the pursuit of his hands. In fact, she'd set her almond eyes on his and purred when he'd cupped her backside, among other parts of her body that he had no business touching. Her purr continued to keep him up all night wondering if she still made the same sound when she was aroused.

A long, cinnamon-hazelnut leg poked out of the bathroom door, followed by the rest of her body. She was wrapped in a white terrycloth towel, and her soft curls were pinned atop her head. Grayson swallowed. Hard.

In all the scenarios he'd played out in his mind, not one of them had Sage exiting the bathroom wearing nothing more than a towel. He briefly noticed the headphones in her ears that were connected to her iPhone. She looked different from the last time he saw her. Curvier. *Sexier.* She pursed her lips together, accentuating her high cheekbones, and danced to whatever music she was listening to. Her skin glistened from her recent shower, and suddenly Grayson was infatuated with the droplets of water running down her collarbone, glistening along the way.

In the back of his mind, he knew he should make his presence known, but there was something so refreshing about admiring her beauty without her knowing. He couldn't believe she hadn't seen him at the end of the hall already. He took a few steps toward her to finally step into her line of vision, but her words stopped him.

"Touch me like I've never been touched before." She dipped her hips and did a little shimmy, bringing his attention to her butt. He titled his head to the side as she repeated the move. *Hmm. Definitely more back there than I remember.* He'd always loved her butt. Perfectly round. Looked great in a pair of jean shorts. But today, it looked so squeezable. Desirable. Even with the concealment of the towel, he noticed the difference.

"Kiss me like I'm the only one that you want." She rolled her hips and did some type of two-step. She was definitely the one he wanted, which of course was why he was here. For years, he'd been comparing his past girlfriends to Sage, which was crazy since he'd never actually dated Sage.

Hell, Tate had threatened to wring his neck for even entertaining the idea of dating Sage. They weren't Romeo and Juliet, but there were definitely a few people from their families who had apparently picked up on their flirtatious ways in the past and hinted that he should stay away from Sage. Even his own sister had told him, *Once a playboy, always a playboy.*

Well, that may have been the case back then, but today, he was a whole new Grayson. Today, he was Grayson Ellington 2.0. The former player who'd finally decided to throw in the towel. He'd actually thrown in the towel a few years ago and only dated one woman at a time. But old rumors died hard, and despite his growth, people in Summerland, Michigan, and an hour away in Ann Arbor, where he currently resided, still labeled him as such.

"Grayson, you're the one I've been waiting for."

His gaze left her butt and flew to the back of her head. *"Grayson, you're the one I've been waiting for"?*

Did she really just put my name in that song? When he heard his name leave her lips again, he couldn't wait for her to notice him any longer.

He cleared his throat, but she still didn't turn around. He didn't want to approach her in case she turned around swinging, so he called out to her from his spot on the wall.

"Sage. I knocked on the door, but no one answered."

She turned around quicker than he had anticipated and yelped in surprise. It only took her a few seconds for recognition to sink in.

"Grayson, what the hell are you doing here?" Her voice was about five notches higher than it had been when she was singing.

"I'm here on business and I forgot you were here and I knocked and no answer so I came up and you were singing so I waited." *Man, what the hell was that? I never talk in run-on sentences.* The Ellington men were known for being smooth talkers. Charmers. So charismatic, a woman couldn't help but want to throw her panties at him.

Judging by the look of irritation on Sage's face and the disbelief reflected in her eyes, he'd say he was proving all those facts to no longer be true. *Come on, Ellington. Do what you came here for.*

"I guess what I'm trying to ask," he said as he took a few steps in her direction, "is would you mind if I took the basement or second-floor bedroom for a few days while I'm here on business?" She didn't say anything, but her eyes held his. "My client has an urgent matter that needs my immediate attention."

She squinted her eyes together. "And your client just so happens to be in the Dominican Republic?"

"The Hendersons are actually right down the street."

"And you have no other motive for wanting to come down here when you knew I would be here?"

He gave her a half smile. "I already told you. I forgot you were here."

"Bullshit."

He shrugged his shoulders. "Maybe."

"Definitely."

"You always did come back at my responses quickly." He took a couple more steps toward her. "That's one of the things I always liked about you."

Sage crossed her arms over her chest and quirked an eyebrow. "Grayson Ulysses Pearson Ellington, the truth, please?"

He winced. "Did you really have to say my entire government name? You know I hate my middle names."

The sly smile that crossed her lips hit him right in the gut.

"You have one minute to tell me why you're really here, or I'm calling my brother, and we both know he won't like you being here with me."

"I'm not afraid of your brother," he said with a laugh. Tate might intimidate a lot of men, but they were about the same size and build. Grayson was pretty sure he could take him in a fight if he needed to. It all depended on what he was fighting for. He was done heeding Tate's warning by staying away from Sage, so if dating her was reason for them to fight, he was prepared to win.

"Maybe not. But I'm sure you still wouldn't want me to call him."

"You're right, I don't want you to call him, but the decision is yours to make." He'd always loved their natural banter; however, now he had to figure out his next move, if she was okay with him staying. The closer he stepped to her, the more aware his body became.

Her eyes widened when he stopped about a foot from her. His studied her eyes and the curves of her face, etching her facial structure in his mind so that he could remember every little detail. He wasn't sure he'd ever met someone with skin as smooth as hers. Unable to help himself, he rubbed her cheek with the back of his hand.

"Still as smooth as silk," he whispered, although he had only meant to think the thought, not speak it out loud. The slow rise and fall of her chest captured his attention, drawing his eyes to the peek of cleavage underneath the towel.

Sage had never been modest around him, although now that he thought about it, she probably should have been. If he didn't step away soon, there was no doubt in his mind that he would do something stupid.

"Okay," she said when he dropped his hand back to his side.

"Okay what?"

She sighed and was the first to step away. "Okay, you can stay on the second floor or in the basement."

Chapter 3

Step away before you do something stupid. Sage was trying her best to calm her nerves, quickly realizing that it was probably a waste of time. *Why in the world didn't I just choose to shower in the master suite bathroom?* Forget the fact that she'd just been in the shower imagining that Grayson was in there with her, doing things that definitely didn't fall into the friend category.

If there was one thing she knew about Grayson, it was that he always had a hidden agenda. It wasn't that he was untrustworthy. Even though they hadn't spoken in years, she trusted him with her life. He was one of her oldest friends, and as a result, she knew that Grayson Ellington did not fly all the way to Punta Cana, Dominican Republic, to meet with a client that she was sure he could meet with in the United States after the holiday.

When she stepped back, he didn't follow her, but he still continued to watch her every move. Granted, she was in a towel, but all her goods were covered, and she never had been a modest person. If he was going to look, she was going to look at her fill of him, too.

Her gaze barely made it off his piercing light brown eyes before landing on his perfectly shaped lips. Lips that she wished she had the courage to kiss right now. That was the problem with being around Grayson. He always made her feel as if she was losing her self-control. Even now, standing there in khaki shorts and a white tee, looking sexier than he had in her dreams, he really irritated her.

How in the world was she supposed to ignore this man when his toffee-colored skin, neatly trimmed goatee and well-defined facial features made her want to sop him up like a buttermilk biscuit?

He had the type of body that demanded every woman's utmost attention, and growing up, he'd definitely gotten hers. Judging from the way her body was responding to him now, he still had her undivided attention. His broad shoulders made her want to climb his body and never get down, while his chiseled arms had her so close to drooling, she subconsciously touched her mouth just to make sure she wasn't. *Whatever woman said that a man who was in his prime at twenty and went downhill after thirty never met thirty-five-year-old Grayson Ellington.*

Just like his dad and uncles, she was sure Grayson was the type of man who only got sexier with age. His light gray hair meshed with his black hair, giving him this salt-and-pepper look that defied words. It was an Ellington male trait and one that Grayson obviously wore very well. His look and aura had a definition all its own. Groomed, yet rugged. Arrogant, but still humble. Protective and submissive when needed. You couldn't buy that type of look out of a box, and you definitely couldn't duplicate it.

When he lightly licked his lips before they curled into a side smile, goose bumps developed all over her arms. *Some things never change,* she thought as she gently shook her head. Was it pathetic to have a crush on a man as undeniably sexy as Grayson? Absolutely not. Was it pitiful to have your crush last for two decades? An irrefutable *yes.*

"I'm going to go change," she said, quickly brushing past him. "You can choose this floor or the basement. It doesn't matter to me."

Just when she thought she was in the clear, she felt his hand on her arm. She immediately stopped walking and glanced at his hand. She didn't have to look at his face to know he felt the heat between them just as much as she did.

"I promise to stay out of your way." His voice was husky. Strained even.

"Okay," she replied, never looking up at his face. He waited a few more seconds before he finally released her arm. When she arrived at the master suite on the third floor, she quickly closed the door and lay on the bed.

"Grayson Ellington is here," she said aloud. "He's actually here in the DR for God knows how long, and no matter what he says, it's not for a business meeting."

She wasn't blind to the attraction they'd been fighting for years, so she knew why he was there. They'd been faced with temptation before, and Grayson had chosen not to pursue her. The more she thought about him being in the Dominican Republic, the more anxiety she felt.

And the longer she sat on the bed, the more she realized that she wasn't nervous about him rejecting her again... She was nervous about the possibility that he wouldn't.

She had six days on the island, and Grayson's appearance had officially messed up her first early morning on vacation. Not only had she been hiding in her room since yesterday evening, but also she'd been forced to eat the snacks she'd brought for her plane ride because she hadn't wanted to leave the solidarity of her room.

Sage unfolded and folded her clothes for the third time this morning. "This is ridiculous," she said to the empty room. "He's your friend. In fact, he's one of your oldest friends. You can't stay hidden in this room forever."

Sage had always been the type of person to face things head-on, but clearly, Grayson was causing her to act out of character. Which wasn't really unusual since he'd been making her feel uncomfortable since she was sixteen years old and just beginning to realize what it meant for a woman to be sexually aroused...

Sixteen years ago

"Sage, are you warm enough?"

She looked up at Grayson and immediately got lost in his light brown eyes. She'd had a crush on him for years, but tonight, standing under a bridge while rain poured down all around them, was making her feel something she'd never felt before. She didn't know exactly what it was, but she felt it nonetheless.

"I'm fine," she replied, snuggling a little closer. "If

I had to get stuck in the rain with someone, I'm glad it's you."

He looked a little surprised by her statement. "Me, too." His hands ran up and down her arms, and the movement warmed her entire body. She wasn't sure why her brother thought it was a good idea for him and Piper to get the car on the other side of the lake, instead of all four of them going—or him and Grayson—but she couldn't complain about her present company.

"How do you like college so far?"

"I like it." He took a few steps back so that he could lean against the pillar. Either that, or he was trying to put some distance between them. She didn't know which.

"What do you like the most?" She adjusted her drenched jean shorts and wrung out the bottom of her top that was plastered to her body. When Grayson didn't respond, she glanced up at him.

His eyes were on her legs, probably oblivious to the fact that she'd asked him a question. It wasn't the first time she'd caught him staring at her legs. He'd been stealing glances at them all day.

"Like what you see?"

"Hmm, what did you say?" he asked, finally bringing his eyes to hers.

"I asked," she said, stepping closer to him, "if you like what you see."

His eyes grew big as they studied hers. "Um, like what I see? What do you mean?"

Sage shot him a look of disbelief. "Seriously? As if I haven't noticed you checking out my legs and chest all day."

"Well, uh…" He stammered over his words, something Grayson never usually did. She wasn't sure why she enjoyed the fact that he was uncomfortable so much, but she did. Maybe it was payback for all those times he made her feel uncomfortable, even if he did so unknowingly.

"Cut out all the flirting," he said when she moved closer to him.

She gave him an innocent smile. "But we flirt all the time."

"Not anymore, we don't."

"Well, I disagree." She curled her body into his as he instinctively wrapped his arms around her. The temperature seemed to drop a few degrees, causing Sage to shiver. Rain she could deal with. A growing thunderstorm was definitely not her cup of tea. She absolutely hated the sound of thunder. It was one of those small fears she'd never grown out of.

"You're okay," Grayson said as he continued to rub his hands up and down her arms just as he had before. She loved that she didn't have to tell him what she needed—he just knew.

"Thanks for always looking out for me." She lifted her head to look him in the eyes, noticing for the first time how close she had inched toward him when the thunder began.

"I'll always look out for you."

Sage wondered if he knew how raspy his voice had gotten when he said that. Her mother always told her if you keep poking at a bear, eventually it would bite back. Well, she wanted Grayson to bite back, and if he didn't bite, she was okay with a little nibble.

She bit her bottom lip as she admired the outline

of his mouth. A mouth she'd wanted to kiss ever since she'd learned that boys didn't really have cooties.

"Sage," he said in a warning tone.

"I can't help it," she said as she licked her lips. "College looks good on you."

He shook his head and briefly looked at the ground. "Like I said, we aren't going there so you better stop flirting with me."

Sage squinted in confusion. "And like I said, we flirt all the time."

"That was then, and it was harmless. This is now."

"Well, clearly someone didn't get the memo." She glanced down at the imprint straining against his jeans.

Grayson looked down at his pants in frustration. "That's just because it's raining outside."

"You expect me to believe that?" she said with a laugh. "I'm pretty sure you should shrivel in the rain, not grow. I don't buy it."

"It doesn't matter if you buy it or not. It's the truth."

She read the determination in his eyes, and she hoped he read the challenge in hers.

"Can we just stand here and keep each other warm until Tate and Piper get back?"

Sage's demeanor softened. He really did sound drained. "Okay," she finally said. "I'll stop flirting with you."

His shoulders slumped in relief. He actually looked more relieved than she'd seen him look all day. "Thank you."

In response, she just smiled as she leaned her head against his chest. Despite the fact that they had agreed not to flirt, the moment still felt extremely romantic. How many nights had she dreamed about being in Grayson's arms? Way more than she could count.

They stood still for a few minutes, wrapped in each other's arms. Sage was so caught up in her thoughts, she barely noticed that Grayson's hands were slowly moving up and down her back until they rested right at the top of her backside.

On more than one occasion, she'd heard Grayson say he was a leg and butt man. Quite frankly, she'd spent careful time picking an outfit that was casual enough for a fishing trip, but accentuated her best features, which happened to be those. She nestled into the crook of his neck and arched her back, hoping that he would take the bait and lower his hands. After a couple more movements on her part, she eventually felt his hands cup her butt.

Jackpot, she thought. It was really unlike her to be quite this bold with a guy, especially Grayson. However, she couldn't help the desire filling her every pore. It was consuming her, and by the rapid rise and fall of his chest, it was obviously consuming him, as well.

"Sage, tell me to remove my hands."

She chanced peering up at him and was so glad she did. His restraint was hanging on by a thin thread, and there was no way she was giving him a lifeline.

He shook his head. "This is wrong, and I'm too old for you."

"Whatever," she said, rolling her eyes. "You haven't even turned nineteen yet, so we're only two years apart."

"More like three, since my birthday is soon, and you're Tate's little sister."

"The way you're making me feel right now is anything but sisterly." She took it one step further and placed a soft kiss on his neck.

"Sage." The warning tone in his voice had returned.

She stood slightly on her tiptoes and leaned into him more, testing his willpower while her lips placed soft kisses along his neck and ears.

"Shit," he said breathlessly when she nibbled, before her tongue slipped out to soothe the small ache. Within seconds, he opened his legs wider and adjusted her body so that she was stationed right in between his legs.

She didn't have much experience flirting with the opposite sex, but she had a feeling she was doing a damn good job if Grayson's reaction was any indication. When she felt his entire body get rigid underneath her hands, she moved away from his neck to peer into his eyes. When hers locked with his, what she saw nearly took her breath away. She'd spent the past fifteen or twenty minutes poking the bear, and apparently, the bear was done playing by her rules.

His mouth crashed on hers quicker than she could calculate as greedy lips met her needy ones. Even with the urgency of his kiss, his tongue was moving in slow methodical movements, and the feelings in the pit of her stomach were swarming like bees around a beehive.

Kissing Grayson while standing together under a bridge with the soothing sound of rain as their own personal soundtrack was exactly what Sage had pictured when she'd imagined her first kiss with Grayson.

His lips softened and the kiss grew slower. He was a masterful kisser, and she had kissed a bunch of frogs just to prepare for this moment that she knew would happen with Grayson.

She ached to get closer to him, but when her hardened nipples brushed against his chest, he suddenly broke the kiss.

He didn't look at her right away, but instead dropped

his head to the ground. "That shouldn't have happened." He lifted his head slowly.

"Speak for yourself," she said when their eyes met. "I've waited way too long to see what you taste like."

His eyes widened. "What has gotten into you?"

Her mouth turned upward in thought. Did he seriously expect her to answer a question so obvious? Well, he was sadly mistaken.

"Oh, come on," she said, playfully swatting him on the arm. "We were bound to kiss. And besides, you're only in town for the weekend, so no harm done. You'll go back to school and forget it even happened."

She, on the other hand, was not going to forget it. There was no way.

Chapter 4

Grayson looked at the digital clock on the microwave before turning his attention back to the bacon he was frying. It was 11:00 a.m., and he hadn't seen Sage since he'd arrived yesterday. He would have thought she'd come out of the bedroom by now, but he guessed she'd rather stay cooped up in the room than deal with the fact that he was here.

He had a plan, though. One of the perks of knowing someone for most of your life. A lot of things might have changed about Sage Langley, but there were also quite a few things that remained the same.

"That smells wonderful," Sage said as she entered the kitchen wearing a blue cotton dress that showed off her amazing toned legs.

"You never could ignore the smell of bacon and cinnamon rolls."

She scrunched her forehead. "I didn't see cinnamon

rolls when I arrived yesterday and took inventory of the stocked food."

Since Tate had originally been scheduled to stay at his vacation home, Grayson had asked a local who often checked on his house when he was away to stock the fridge with food for Tate and his girlfriend, Olivia.

"I went and picked up a few of your favorite foods earlier this morning."

She crossed her arms over her chest. "How can you be so sure that you still know what my favorites are? It's literally been almost a decade since you cooked me anything."

He smiled, but continued to fry the bacon rather than turn to her. "I know you love cinnamon rolls, but only paired with bacon. You like orange juice with pulp, but you like to use a strainer to remove the pulp before you drink it because you swear it tastes better than plain orange juice. You don't eat many sweets, but you absolutely can't live without Oreo cookies dipped in peanut butter."

He glanced over his shoulder and observed the unfazed look on her face before continuing. "Cooked carrots make you gag. Broccoli makes you salivate. No one can cook fried pork chops as well as your grandmother did, except for you. White wine is your first choice. Pink wine is your second. But nothing beats a frozen margarita, and you tell everyone that your favorite liquor for shots is vodka when it's actually tequila."

"No, it isn't," she interjected as she took a seat at the table. "Vodka is always my first choice."

Grayson placed the bacon on a plate next to the cinnamon rolls and brought both plates to the table he had already set. "I don't know why you always say vodka is your drink of choice when a margarita is your favorite drink."

"That's true, but I still prefer vodka."

"Wrong again," he said, shaking his head. "Whether you're at a lounge or wedding or any other event that's serving liquor, you always order a margarita for your first drink and a tequila sunrise as your last drink. For the life of me, I never understood why the first shot you ever get is vodka, and when it goes down too rough, which is almost always, you wait a while before you order another shot, and that second choice is always tequila."

Grayson started eating his food, well aware of the look of surprise plastered across Sage's face. After observing him for a few more seconds, she finally began eating.

"What are your plans today?" she asked in between bites.

"If you're interested, I actually thought I could show you some of the island today. I don't have to meet with my client yet."

She continued to look down at her plate and wouldn't meet his eyes.

"You don't have to spend the day with me. I just thought it would be nice to catch up. We haven't really spent any time together since you've been back in the States." He didn't add the fact that he really missed her and wanted nothing more than to hear all about her experiences while she was overseas. He was trying not to sound too desperate.

"I guess that would be okay," she finally answered. "You're right. It's been a long time since we spent any time together as just *friends*."

He didn't miss her emphasis on the word. Since he'd arrived yesterday, Sage seemed to be making it clear that she wanted them to remain in the friend zone.

"Did you tell Tate I was here?"

She finally looked up from her plate. "No. I don't see any reason why he has to know."

Grayson didn't try to hide the smile that crept across his face. To anyone who didn't know Sage, her actions would seem to prove that she wasn't interested. But it was the little things that gave her away. It was the goose bumps that developed on her arms whenever they were near, like yesterday in the hallway and right now sitting at the table. It was in the way her nipples hardened underneath her dress, and the most tell-all sign—she hadn't called her brother. Which meant she didn't want him to know they were together any more than he did.

"Perfect," he said as he thought about the day he had planned. Sage was in for a rude awakening if she thought he was okay with keeping their relationship in the friend zone.

"Where exactly are we going?"

Grayson glanced over at Sage before turning his eyes back to the road. "I was wondering how long it would be before you asked me."

"When you asked me to wear a bathing suit and bring an extra pair of clothes just in case, I assumed you would supply the information, but you didn't."

He smirked as they continued to drive through the Dominican Republic countryside. "That's not exactly how it happened. I would have told you where we were going, had you not escaped out of the kitchen so fast."

She shifted in her seat. "Only because you said I only had an hour to get ready."

He couldn't help but laugh, because they both knew her focus had been less on where they were going and more on the fact that breakfast had been a little awkward. *Maybe I shouldn't have let on how much I remember about her?* He shook his head the minute the thought entered his mind. He couldn't apologize for how he felt, and if anything, he needed to get her accustomed to the idea that they were definitely more than just old friends.

"First, I'm taking you to Macao Beach. Then we're headed to Samana, a province of the Dominican Republic."

Even in his peripheral, he could see her forehead crease in thought. He was sure she would have remained silent during the remainder of the trip had they not stopped at a location off the road.

"Um, what exactly is this place?" Sage asked after he turned off the car.

"It's a tourist spot," he said as he got out of the car and went around to the passenger side to open the door for Sage. She glanced around at all the auto pieces scattered on the property, and Grayson tried his best not to laugh. It definitely looked more like a junkyard than a tourist spot.

"Grayson, my friend," a man said eagerly as he exited the building. "I heard you were in town, but I didn't believe it."

"Hey, Samson." Grayson returned his handshake. "Yeah, I have some business to attend to while I'm here. I'd like to introduce you to Sage Langley." He placed his hand on the small of her back. "Sage is visiting the Dominican Republic for the first time, and I was hoping you had two dune buggies we can borrow for a few hours."

Sage's face flew to Grayson. "Dune buggies like we did back when we took that trip to Myrtle Beach?"

"Yeah, we had a lot of fun during that trip, and I figured it's been a while since you drove one."

"Not since that trip," she said with excitement. "Thanks for planning this." She studied his eyes with a soft smile that was full of intrigue and surprise. He always did love to surprise her, even though he didn't get to nearly as much as he wanted. Even when they were teenagers, he'd do little things to surprise her, like pick up candy for her when he and Tate went to the store.

"Ah," Samson interrupted. "Now I see why you really came back to the Dominican Republic." Samson's voice broke the trance, and Sage dropped her eyes to the dirt ground.

"I definitely have a couple buggies for you, and our second tour group just arrived back, so we already have buggies ready to go." Samson looked to Sage. "The actual tour group building is about two blocks down the road. This is where we build and fix the buggies."

Sage nodded her head in understanding. After a quick drive down the road, fifteen minutes of prep and a quick lesson, they were ready to go. Unlike other tourists, Grayson didn't need a guide to tell him how to get around the island. There'd been a period in his life when he was in the Dominican Republic almost as much as he was in the United States.

"Are you sure you're okay riding in your own buggy, or do you want to ride with me?"

She shot him a big smile. "I'm fine on my own,

thanks." There she was. That was the Sage he knew. The one who was always down for some fun and eager to prove she could handle whatever a man could. He was glad she had chosen to wear a long teal skirt and white tank, because even though she looked amazing, her legs were concealed, so at least he wouldn't have that distraction until they got to the beach.

"Then let's get this party started." As they began their journey to Macao Beach, it wasn't the scenery that he was looking forward to showing Sage; it was the community they would have to drive through before arriving at the beach.

It was finally time for the first step in his plan to save the modern-day Scrooge in flip-flops.

Chapter 5

Sage was thoroughly enjoying driving the dune buggy through the Dominican Republic countryside. There was something so soothing about cruising down the narrow road and soaking in the scenery and atmosphere.

However, she knew the landscape wasn't the only thing exciting her. It had been years, literally years, since a man had cared enough about her to plan to spend an entire day together. The fact that he had started their morning with preparing her favorite breakfast food in the entire world was enough to make her weak in the knees. She had no idea he remembered that much about her, nor did she realize he even knew her likes and dislikes in the first place.

What's his angle? There were a lot of things she knew about Grayson Ellington, but the man who she was with now didn't exactly fit the Grayson she remembered.

Her thoughts were halted when they approached a row of houses and a few small stores. Within seconds of passing the first house, kids began filing out of every one. Since Grayson was in the leading buggy, she observed what he did and then followed suit. It seemed most of the kids were happy to high-five them as they drove by, as if this was the most excitement they'd had all day. When they neared the middle of the row of houses, Grayson pulled over.

"Why are we stopping?" Sage asked as Grayson walked to her buggy. He studied her face, but she wasn't quite sure what he was looking for. He glanced behind her, and she turned around to see what he was looking at and giggled. All the kids were running toward them.

"Come with me real quick," he said, taking her hand and helping her out of the buggy. They only took a few steps before they reached the edge of one of the small stores.

"We stopped in El Macao because I want to show you this." When they stepped behind the store, Sage gasped in surprise.

"Oh, wow," she said, placing her hand over her heart. "This is really remarkable." In the middle of the backyard of the store, standing what seemed to be about eight feet tall, was a Christmas tree made of beer bottles.

As they walked closer, Sage was really able to admire the artistry behind the tree. "I've never seen anything like it."

"That's because no one has talents like I do," said a young man as he approached. "Grayson, my man, thanks for the call. I'm so glad you're back in town."

Grayson and the young man pounded fists. "Sage,

I'd like to introduce you to Jose. He's the creative mind behind this masterpiece. Jose, this is Sage."

"It's nice to meet you, Sage," he said, extending a hand.

"It's nice to meet you, too," she said, returning his handshake. "How in the world did you come up with this idea?"

Jose smiled before responding. "We like to celebrate Christmas in this town, but growing up, we could never afford Christmas trees. But it's easy to pick up bottles that clutter the street. I started collecting bottles when I was ten to sell them at a place that gives you money for glass bottles, so that I could buy Christmas gifts for my siblings and others in the neighborhood. Grayson was here visiting around that time, and I told him that what I really wanted was to bring the Christmas spirit to this town and do something for everyone. I'm not sure what clicked when we talked, but I got this idea and have been building this Christmas tree ever since."

Sage nodded. "Do what you can with what you have."

"Exactly," Jose said. "Now I'm a youth advocate in Santo Domingo, the capital city of Dominican Republic, but I come back every year to build this tree. It gets larger each year, and people in the community and regular vacationers who used to not visit our small town come through just to see the tree. It's really helped the morale in this place."

Sage couldn't help but get mushy. Despite the fact that she didn't care for Christmas, she admired Jose and the way he instilled happiness in the community with the resources he had.

"I'm truly impressed," she said to Jose. "The message behind the tree is just as amazing as the tree itself."

"Thank you, Ms. Sage." Jose glanced at Grayson before turning back to Sage. "Okay, kids, you can come on around." All of a sudden, all the little kids that Sage had seen when they first entered the town came running around the corner, jumping up and down.

"Here you go," Grayson said, handing a black bag to Sage. "Start passing out one of each."

She looked at him in confusion until she peeked in the bag and found coloring books and crayons in there. She hadn't even noticed the black bags before, and she was usually really observant.

The kids were anxious to get ahold of the coloring books and crayons, each hugging her leg, arm or whatever they could when she passed them out. After they'd distributed the goodies, they played and chatted with the kids for thirty more minutes.

Sage was fluent in Spanish, Mandarin and French, but she had forgotten that Grayson was fluent in Spanish, as well. That realization was another reminder of just how long it had been since they'd spent quality time together.

"Thank you both so much for stopping through," Jose said when Grayson and Sage were getting ready to leave. "A lot of these kids won't get any gifts for Christmas, so I know they really appreciate it."

"Don't mention it," Grayson said as he helped Sage into the buggy. "I spoke with Samson, and he will be bringing by a truckload of gifts the day before Christmas that we were able to buy after the Thanksgiving fund-raiser I had last month for this community. And he's working with a few other communities, as well."

Jose's eyes lit up. "That's amazing. I forgot you even had the fund-raiser."

As the men chatted, Sage took the moment to observe Grayson and how he interacted with the townspeople. Here she was, harping on past experiences and letting it taint her view of Christmas, while the kids at El Macao remained excited about the holiday even though they usually didn't have presents to open. She couldn't help but reflect on the true meaning of Christmas and question if it was her past that made her dislike the holiday, or if somewhere along the line, she'd forgotten what the holiday was truly about.

"You're quiet."

Sage turned toward Grayson and offered a small smile. "Sorry." She glanced around Macao Beach and sighed at the beauty in front of her. "This beach is gorgeous."

"It is," Grayson said with a smile. "It's one of the few public beaches that isn't overtaken by tourists. Even though a lot of tours stop at this beach, they usually only stay for a short while and then they move on."

When her feet hit the crème-colored sand, she immediately removed her flips-flops just as Grayson removed his shoes. Today, he was wearing a beige shirt and russet swim trunks that looked perfect against his creamy complexion. A part of her was glad he was here, while another part was nervous about the consequences of his visit. He had no idea how many times she had missed his company when she was overseas.

"You see that area over there?" Sage followed the direction of his hand.

"Yes."

"That's where we're headed." They walked in silence for a few more steps. Being around him felt so natural, as if it hadn't been years since they were with one another.

"Why didn't you ever call while you were overseas?"

Sage glanced to the right to look at Grayson. "I called."

He gave a quick side smile. "Not a lot, and when you did, it was always for just a few minutes."

Is he serious? Did he remember the last time they were together...truly together? "You know why I didn't call that much, Grayson, and the phone works both ways."

"We talked in the beginning," he said firmly. "But after a while, you never seemed to want to talk to me. So I eventually stopped and left the ball in your court."

"Is that what this trip is about? Or the reason we stopped in El Macao to give gifts to the kids?" She waved her hands in the air. "Let me guess. This trip was your way of trying to leave a good memory of yourself with me for Christmas in hopes of replacing the bad one."

"Whoa, that's not it," he said as he lightly touched her arm so she would stop walking. "I thought we both agreed that night that we were better off as friends. I wasn't trying to leave a bad memory for you years ago during the holidays, when I of all people know what you went through."

The vein in his neck pulsed, which always seemed to happen when he was frustrated. Whether he'd gotten into an argument with his dad or lost a basketball game, that vein was always a dead giveaway at how frustrated he was. Suddenly, observing that vein was a lot better than dealing with the conversation she knew they needed to have.

"Sage, stop looking at my neck," he said, interrupting her thoughts and proving once again just how well he knew her.

"Can we not do this?" she asked breathlessly.

Grayson's eyes softened, and he took another step toward her. "Listen, you have to stop running." He took her bag off her shoulder and placed it on the sand next to the book bag he'd brought along. "When was the last time you let it all out?"

Please don't do this. She didn't want to talk. She didn't need to talk. The only thing she needed to do was walk to those rocks he'd pointed at and take a seat to calm the anxiety slowly creeping up her spine.

"I'm fine," she said as she closed her eyes. "I'm fine." She repeated the words a few more times before she opened her eyes to find Grayson still standing near, observing her. Analyzing her. No doubt trying to study her body language before saying whatever he wanted to say next.

"I don't believe you." He picked up both bags and continued toward the rocks that were only a few feet away. "Until we talk about the reason you stayed out of the country for eight years, we'll never get past it."

Her irritation shot through her body like quicksand. "We'll never get through this? Who the hell are you?" she yelled. Her heart was racing, and she was glad the only other people on the beach were so far away they were out of earshot.

"We aren't a couple. We've never dated. We haven't talked in years except for that forced conversation we had at Piper's wedding, and the occasional small talk when I ran into you and my brother when I got back to the States."

He stopped walking and placed both bags back in the

sand. "This is why we need to talk. I'm sorry for how I handled things when you told me how you felt that Christmas you came into town, before Piper got married. I even found you to fix it, but you didn't want to have anything to do with me. I handled it terribly, and what I should have told you was that I was feeling the exact same thing you were feeling."

"You do not get to do this," she said, pointing at him. "It's been years since we had that conversation, and I had been so excited that holiday to tell my family about my teaching experience so far. That was the first Christmas I had celebrated with them in a long time, and you ruined it for me."

"I know," he said, stepping to her. "I was an idiot, and if I'm the reason you stayed away from your family for the past few years during the holidays, I'm so sorry for ever doing that to you."

"That's the only time you're apologizing for?" She took a couple steps back as her frustration rose. "What about apologizing for asking me to accompany you on that trip to California, showing me an amazing time, kissing me like I was the only woman in your life and then treating me as if I didn't exist?"

Too many years she'd spent imagining a future with a man who didn't want her. A schoolgirl crush that had escalated into the most meaningful relationship she'd had in her entire life.

"Sage, I can't apologize enough for what I've done in the past, but I'm trying to focus on the present in hopes for a future with you."

"Oh, that's just great," she said sarcastically as she held in unshed tears. "I guess now that you've realized we should be together, I should just forget about how you hurt me."

She turned to face the water and closed her eyes. The sun was starting to set, and she couldn't even relish the beauty of the moment. When she felt Grayson's arms reach around her waist, she couldn't help but lean into him for support.

He was always that person for her. The same man who could make her so angry that she felt as if she could scream in frustration was the exact same man who could calm her down even better than her brothers, mother or Piper could.

"It hurts me to the core to have to think about the issues I've developed from years of being rejected by you," she said in the calmest voice she could muster. Sometimes, honesty was the best policy, and it didn't get more honest than that.

"I was a jackass more than once. That I'll admit. And it's okay to blame me for all your trust issues." He hugged her a little tighter. "But we both know that what your father did is also part of the root of the problem, and you definitely don't give me excuses for my actions, so it's time for you to stop giving him excuses and cope with what he did to your family."

Chapter 6

Stop giving him excuses, and cope with what he did to your family. Grayson thought about the last words he'd said to Sage and wished he could slap himself across the face.

When he'd thought about the day, that was definitely not what he had planned. It was his fault for asking her why she'd never called him when she was overseas. He'd opened up a can of worms when all he'd wanted to do today was show her that he cared.

He had canceled their plans in Samana, knowing that the pleasant mood for the day had been killed. She didn't even speak the entire ride home after they dropped off the dune buggies.

He rolled over in bed and glanced at the clock. It was 2:00 a.m., and he hadn't gotten a wink of sleep. On nights like this, the only thing that worked for him was a shot of bourbon or some hot tea. Since he didn't particularly enjoy drinking alone, hot tea won.

Tiptoeing as much as possible, he made his way down the stairs to the first floor. He hadn't even made it entirely into the kitchen when he noticed Sage looking out the window at the ocean. She was holding a mug that he'd bet was filled with tea, and she was wearing a robe, which did nothing to stop his imagination. The moon cascaded across her face, illuminating her delicate features. *She is so extremely beautiful.* And for him, it was that hit-you-in-the-head type of beauty. The kind that made men question every woman they'd been with before her, because her beauty shined inside and out.

He knew how crazy it seemed to her, but if he'd learned anything today, it was that he definitely did love her. Of course, he'd always loved her, and he suspected that she was in love with him, but now he was pretty sure that he was *deeply* in love with her.

It really didn't make sense to him, either. To be in love with the woman she was in the past and to look forward to loving the woman she would be in the future, but to have the strongest feelings for the woman she was now, when technically he hadn't been around her for years, seemed a bit contrived.

He thought about all the times his aunt had said that true love didn't have to make sense, it only had to feel right. Well, loving Sage definitely felt right. Now the only thing he needed to do was get her to love him back.

"I didn't know you were down here," he said, making his presence known. She only slightly tilted her head in his direction before turning back to the window. He cautiously walked toward her, unsure if he should make his tea or just head back to his room and let her be alone.

"Are you just going to stand there all night, or are you going to fix yourself a cup of hot tea to help you sleep? The pot is already on the stove." She finally looked over at him. "Or did you come down for a shot of bourbon instead?"

He smiled, loving the fact that she still remembered what helped him get to sleep. "I think I'll have tea."

After he fixed his tea, they sat in comfortable silence, both caught up in their own thoughts. When Sage placed her empty mug in the sink, she was almost out the door when she spoke to him.

"Can I ask you a question?"

"You can ask me anything."

She walked back to where he was sitting. "What did you mean when we were on the beach and you said you even found me to try to fix it, but I didn't want anything to do with you? The next time we spoke after that Christmas was Piper's wedding, and when we did chat, you didn't say anything."

Crap. He hadn't even realized he'd let that slip.

"I didn't say anything at Piper's wedding because I hadn't gone after you yet."

She squinted in confusion. "What do you mean?"

He sighed, wishing again that the day could have gone drama-free. It wasn't his proudest moment, so he definitely didn't want to bring it up.

"I went to Barcelona six months after Piper's wedding, when you first started teaching there, to tell you that I was sorry and that I'd made a mistake. Then I saw you grading papers at a table outside of that café connected to the building you had lived in at the time.

You had on this red dress that I'm sure was supposed to look casual, but it was so sexy on you."

Sage lifted her head and her eyes grew bigger with every word he said, but he forced himself to continue.

"You looked so adorable that day. Your hair cascaded around your shoulders and whipped gently in the wind. You looked so content. Worry-free." He smiled slightly, caught up in the memory. "I must have stood there and stared at you for thirty minutes, or maybe even an hour. I'm surprised someone didn't approach me about how creepy I probably looked."

She shook her head, and for a moment, he thought she was going to say that she didn't believe him.

"I remember that day," she said, her voice barely a whisper. "I had felt like someone was watching me."

"I know," he said with a laugh.

"And I'd even looked directly at the spot where I felt like the person was standing and didn't see anyone."

"I know that, too, because I sat down at a table across the street with my back turned toward you when you began searching."

She shook her head with a smile. "How did you even know I was in Barcelona? There's no way Tate would have told you, and since I was only in Barcelona for a couple months, I didn't post anything on social media."

"Piper told me."

"I should have known she would help you."

"You know she's always been a sucker for a good romance story."

"She has," Sage agreed. "Do you remember that summer when she went to that drama camp and landed a starring role?"

"Oh, yeah," he said, snapping his fingers. "She made

Tate practice with her the whole day before the show, and when they had to do that kissing scene, she quoted a line from Shakespeare right after their kiss."

Sage laughed. "She did, and Tate didn't know what to say or do. I've never seen my brother speechless, but that day, he honestly didn't know what to do with Piper."

"He's been speechless before. What about Piper's wedding?"

She nodded. "You're right. At Piper's wedding, he barely said anything to anyone."

"I know it was hard for him." He took another sip of his tea. "He never told me how he felt about Piper, but I can imagine watching a girl you care about marry someone else isn't a good feeling."

Sage began twirling her fingers in circles on the kitchen table. She only did that when something was on her mind that she wanted the answer to, but didn't want to ask.

"What is it?"

She looked up from the table, and even in the darkness he could see her hesitance. "Did Tate ever tell you to stay away from me? You know, not to date me?"

Grayson studied her eyes, unsure of what he should say. Sage was the woman he cared deeply about and wanted a future with, but Tate was his best friend, and there was a certain code that he felt was in play.

"You know Tate. He only wants what's best for you, and always has."

"So in other words, that's a yes. He asked you to stay away from me. It doesn't matter whether you tell me or not. I've always known he probably did."

"He's just concerned about you, that's all."

Sage leaned back in her chair, still fiddling with the

table. "I guess maybe I should have told him to stay away from Piper. She's married, and they're too flirty sometimes."

"No use."

Sage quirked an eyebrow. "Why not?"

"Well, even though I can't stand her husband, the real reason it's no use is because you wouldn't be able to keep them away from one another any more than he'd be able to keep us away from each other." This trip was a prime example of exactly what he meant.

"I suppose you're right."

"Yep. Now, what else is it that you want to ask me?"

She gave him a soft smile, and Grayson assumed it was because he was picking up on the signs that she still had more to ask. She really shouldn't be surprised. He picked up on everything about her.

"Why didn't you approach me in Barcelona that day?" she finally asked. "Why come all that way just to watch me from a distance?"

He tensed immediately. *Man, I've tried to forget that day.* "You don't remember what happened?"

Sage scrunched her forehead in thought. "Not particularly."

"Anything that day?"

"What happened?"

He twisted his neck that was slowly growing tighter. Even though it was years ago, they'd never spoken about it, so sometimes it felt as if it hadn't even happened.

"Just tell me. The longer you wait, the more your neck will tense."

Here goes. "That was the day you received the call from your mother."

At first, Sage looked confused. Then, second by second, he watched the memory come flooding back.

"That was the day my mother called to tell me what my father had done."

Sage felt all the blood rush to her head the minute she said the words. She dropped her head back and closed her eyes, practicing those breathing techniques her therapist had told her about.

She let out a forced laugh at the irony of it all. There was a point in time, when she was a little girl, that she had wanted to be a psychiatrist, but after what happened, there was no way she could counsel anybody.

"I figured you blocked out that memory." Tate leaned over and captured her hand in his. "I'm sorry for bringing it up."

"It's fine. I'm the one who asked." She lifted her head back up and opened her eyes. "I still don't understand why you didn't approach me."

"Tate had called me at the same time your mom called you." His jaw twitched. "I had to watch the emotions flow over your face, and Tate told me he was with your mom. I heard her talking in the background and knew instantly that she was talking to you."

"Did you tell Tate you were in Barcelona?"

"No, I didn't. He told me he was going to fly to Barcelona to be with you, but I guess you told your mom you were going to fly home right away."

"I went home to pack a bag and got on a plane a few hours later." She looked into his eyes. "But you already know that."

Grayson nodded. "Tate called about thirty minutes after you left and told me that you had a three-hour layover in Miami, and asked if my brother could head to the airport to check on you. I was already at the Barcelona airport and lied and told him I'd arrived in Miami that morning, and that I would check on you instead."

Oh, my goodness. Sage's hand flew to her mouth as she finally remembered seeing Grayson that day.

He squeezed her hand a little tighter. "I was able to make a flight out of Barcelona to Miami right after I got Tate's second call, and you arrived a couple hours later."

"I remember…" Her voice trailed off.

Grayson brought his chair closer to hers, still holding her hands. "Sage, it's not that I didn't want to say anything to you in Barcelona. I kept quiet because you needed to deal with what was going on with your family, and if you knew I was there, you would have wanted to know why I'd come. My mom left us when I was ten years old. You know I haven't seen her since she walked right out that front door after she told me we were going to play hide-and-seek, and that I had to be the one to find her."

Grayson took a deep breath. "I searched for her for about an hour or so before my dad got home with my younger siblings and asked where my mother was. I understand what it's like to have a parent not cut out for parenthood. It wasn't fair to you, your brothers or your mom, but your father's mistakes are not your burdens to carry."

She heard what he was saying, but every time she thought about it, her heart ached to a degree she couldn't handle. She barely felt the few tears that were running down her cheeks. Grayson softly brushed those tears away.

She had only gone to five therapy sessions before

she'd decided that she didn't need a therapist. Honestly, she wasn't sure if it was her pride or fear that had caused her to stop her sessions, but she knew she had been running for too long.

Chapter 7

"I run from my problems," she said as she released his hands and brought her knees to her chest. If she was going to talk and get it out, his touch would just turn her to mush. "Not all problems, but anything that reminds me of my father is what I usually choose to forget or ignore. My father was still around when you first moved to Summerland, so you already know I was a daddy's girl.

"You probably also remember hearing stories about how much I used to love Christmas. My parents never had a lot, but my dad always made me feel like his little princess." She even remembered her mom letting her and her brothers open up one gift each a week before Christmas.

"I think my family as a whole just ignored my dad's drug use, especially me. In my eyes, he could do no wrong. Some days he was happy, which were probably the days he was high on something. Other days, he was depressed, which were probably the days nothing was in his system. I didn't think about the fact that he could barely hold a consistent job while my mom worked three jobs to support us. The only bill my dad was in charge of paying was the mortgage. On the Christmas right after I'd turned twelve, our house got repossessed and we learned our payments had been behind for over a year. Even worse, my dad had gotten fired from his job as a snowplow driver in the next town over months ago, and apparently had been busy in the drug scene in Detroit. We hadn't even known he'd been driving to Detroit. We thought he'd been going to work."

Sage knew that Grayson had probably heard this story from her brother, but she still knew she had to finish letting it all out.

"My dad had found a wooden shack in the forest preserve where we would always go play. Really only Isaac and I played there because Tate always claimed he was too old to play in a small wooden house. When the police arrived at our house to tell my mom about all the different things my father was being charged for, I remember listening at the bottom of the stairs, before racing out the back door to the shack I knew my dad might be at to see if what I'd heard was true.

"When I found him there, he was with some woman and they were stuffing cash and drugs into a black bag. I was so surprised by what I saw that I screamed. Within seconds, my dad grabbed me and before I knew it, they were taping my mouth and throwing me into the trunk of some car that I'd never seen before."

Sage felt her body begin to shake at the memory and frustration of the whole ordeal, but she refused to cry about it anymore. She'd shed years of tears over that experience, so instead of waterworks, she grew angry.

"What are you thinking? Keep talking aloud," Grayson said when she'd been quiet too long.

"I'm pissed," Sage continued. "I'm pissed that he had the audacity to actually kidnap me. It was five days, Grayson. Five days of being with him and that slut in some hole-in-the-wall place in some town I didn't know as they plotted to leave the state. And the worst thing about the entire experience is not even the fact that he kidnapped me. It's the fact that even though they tied me up and didn't harm me physically, they broke my spirit, and in a sense, stole the rest of my adolescence."

She glanced out at the moon, thinking about how horrible those days had been. "During the entire five days he didn't even acknowledge that he had a wife or sons, and apparently I wasn't his daughter, either." Her voice grew lower. "His eyes were cold and empty. He'd looked at me with such irritation, probably because I had gone to the shack and he'd felt like the only choice was to take me. They made me pick up after their mess and help them count the money and even separate the drugs into different piles. So, no, I wasn't his daughter that day. I was just a means to an end, and all the great memories I had from my childhood with my father faded away in five long days."

She still remembered when police were stopping people on expressways coming in and out of Michigan, and even with their disguises, an officer had asked them to open the trunk. He immediately recognized her from the news. After the rescue, her family had changed their last name from Stockmen to Langley, her mother's maiden name, to disassociate themselves with her father. They probably would have even left town, but her mother had gotten a lot of support from the townspeople after the rumors subsided. Unfortunately, kids didn't forget as easily.

"I'm even more pissed that he had the nerve to overdose on drugs while he was in jail, when his ass should have rotted in prison for all the stuff he'd been doing for years behind our backs, and for kidnapping me."

Her brothers and mom never mentioned if they'd visited her father in jail. She assumed they didn't want to bring it up, to remind her what had happened. When she'd gotten the call in Barcelona that her father had overdosed, she couldn't really recall what emotion she'd felt first. Anger. Disappointment. Disgust. Relief... Probably a combination of them all.

"My father, the man who was supposed to love and protect me from all the harm in the world, is the same man who, to this day, has caused me more pain than I can ever imagine."

"Come here," Grayson said as he pulled her chair closer to him, lifted her with ease and placed her on his lap. She laid her head on his shoulder as if they'd sat like this a thousand times before.

"What your father did didn't break you as a person, and it definitely doesn't define you as a person, either."

She glanced up at him as she realized something else. "I never told my therapist the entire story, and quite frankly, I've never retold it out loud...only in my head."

He smiled as he gently brushed his hand over her cheek. "I'm always here whenever you need to get out your thoughts. You keep too much bottled up inside, and that's not healthy."

She nodded in agreement. "Thank you for being

there that day in the Miami airport. When I'd gotten the news of my father's death, I really needed someone to hold me, and despite how crazy we probably looked, I'm so grateful that you were there to listen to me rant about my feelings, and I'm so sorry I forgot that moment had happened. You're right, talking about it does help."

Sometimes, she shocked herself with how many thoughts she chose to bottle up and forget about. She'd been doing it for so long that it was often hard to separate fiction from real life because she'd had to concoct stories about what really happened to her father to avoid the harsh realities she would face if people found out who he was.

As she sat there, gazing into Grayson's eyes, she finally understood the harm she was doing to herself. She had to accept what she'd gone through as being a part of her, but not something that defined her, in order to have others truly accept the person she was. Hiding never solved anything, and running definitely didn't help. In her career and other aspects of her life, she was a take-charge person, the true definition of an ambitious go-getter, who'd stop at nothing to prove to others and herself that there wasn't anything she couldn't accomplish.

Grayson may have made some mistakes in the past when she'd expressed her feelings for him, but she wasn't lacking in her mistakes, either. He was always there for her even if she didn't want him to be.

This moment marked the time when she would stop living in the past and start living in the present. She wasn't sure how many women would be in close living quarters with a man like Grayson without taking advantage of the situation, so she had a choice to make.

She could work on rebuilding their friendship, just like Grayson had been trying to do for the past couple days. Or she could give in to the temptation and see if he really did taste as delicious as she remembered.

His eyes sparked with awareness, obviously feeling the same thing she was. She lifted her hand to his face and gently rubbed the pad of her thumb to his lips. *Soft. Smooth. Appetizing.* Lips like Grayson's were made for kissing, among other naughty things that were suddenly clouding her mind.

Sage and Grayson had always connected on not just a physical level, but also mentally and spiritually. She didn't know how to describe the hold he had on her, nor did she understand why the disappointing events that occurred in their lives often brought them to each other and connected them in a mesmerizing way.

He dropped his gaze to her lips in one slow perusal, the hunger in his eyes intensifying.

"Sage, after the talk we just had, maybe you should go to bed and rest up for the day I have planned tomorrow."

She laughed as her hand moved from his lips to outline his face, memorizing every sexy angle. "So you don't really have a meeting here, do you?"

"No," he said with a smile. "I came here for the chance to finally get you all to myself."

Her breath caught at the sincerity reflected in his eyes, but she wasn't blind. The most prominent emotion in his gaze was lust—pure unexploited lust. Mind made up, there was no turning back.

"No more waiting," she whispered before slanting her lips over his.

Eight years ago

"That was an amazing event."

Grayson glanced over at Sage, who was spread across the sofa in the high-rise condo. "It was. Thanks for coming with me. Everyone at the company really liked you."

Sage lifted herself onto her elbows. "You work with some great people, and the cruise was amazing."

He smiled. "It was my first evening cruise in San Fran, but honestly, I wouldn't have enjoyed it as much if you hadn't joined me."

Although he lived and worked in Michigan, he was glad to be at his firm's headquarters in San Francisco. He'd only be here for the summer, but he was even more thrilled when he got the call from Sage to say she was visiting a friend she'd met overseas who was in San Francisco. He'd wasted no time asking her to accompany him to his business event.

His phone dinged for the sixth time in the past hour, and he knew who it was before he even glanced at the screen. When he read the message, he frowned.

"Is that my brother again?"

"Yeah. He saw that picture of us on Facebook, and now he's upset that I didn't tell him you were dropping by to see me while you were in Cali."

Sage rolled her eyes. "He knows better than to send me those messages. I told him when I dropped by his place that I would probably visit you."

Grayson placed his phone back on the counter and ignored Tate's text. He'd already apologized and said he'd make sure he got her back to her friend's place safely. But he knew the real reason Tate was freaking out. Ever since he'd picked up on their attraction years ago, Tate had warned Grayson to stay away from Sage.

And he'd tried…so hard! It seemed even being miles apart in another country didn't stop him from thinking about her. The last girl he'd dated hadn't even met Sage, but she broke up with him because she said his heart wasn't with her…it was with someone else. He didn't have to ask himself who that someone was. She was propped on the couch, still wearing her stunning black dress, staring at him with the sexiest pair of bedroom eyes he'd ever seen.

"Do you want to watch a movie?" Sage asked. "Just like old times."

He thought about the times they'd watched movies in the past. Usually, those times included Tate and Piper.

"Sure." He glanced at her dress again. "Do you want to borrow a pair of sweats and a T-shirt?"

"Yes, please."

He went to the bedroom to grab her a pair of clothes to change into. When he turned around, he found her waiting at the door for him. His words momentarily caught in his throat. They hadn't kissed in eight years, and back then, they'd been teenagers. It seemed light-years away from the twenty-four- and twenty-seven-year-olds they were now.

"Would this work?" He held up the shirt and pants. As she sashayed toward him, he considered that maybe he should have tossed the items to her instead.

"This is perfect," she said, taking the clothes out of his hand. She was standing close to him. Too close. He couldn't breathe when she was this close, because then her scent would fill his nostrils, and that definitely wouldn't work.

"Great." He grabbed some sweats and a T-shirt for himself before quickly exiting the room. Once he had, he went straight to the kitchen to pour himself a glass of ice water. Man, he was really going to have a tough time watching a movie if he was hard as a rock. He had to get himself under control.

"What time are you going back to your friend's place?" he yelled from the kitchen as he quickly discarded his dress clothes and put on his sweatpants.

"Did I forget to tell you?"

He stopped right in the middle of putting on his T-shirt. "Tell me what?"

Sage walked out of the bedroom looking even sexier in his clothes than she had in her dress. He let out a long breath, although he definitely hadn't meant to. The look on her face proved she'd heard him.

"I told my friend Crystal that I wouldn't be returning tonight and would see her at her place in the morning."

His heart started beating a mile a minute. "Um, is that because you're staying here?"

Sage shot him an innocent look. "Of course I am, silly."

His thoughts were racing as he finished putting on his shirt. What did this mean? How was he supposed to deal with her being in the same vicinity as him for extended hours and not be tempted to touch her?

"I'll make the popcorn," Sage said, not waiting for him to respond. Things were happening too fast for him to calculate. They hadn't even picked out what movie they were going to watch. He could sense when Sage had a hidden agenda, but the biggest question on his mind was, how far was he going to take this? When Sage set her mind to something, she usually accomplished it, and right now, that determined look was pinned on him.

And he had a feeling he was in for a few more surprises.

An hour into the movie and Grayson was fighting a losing battle. He considered himself a strong man with great willpower. He'd been involved with his fair share of beautiful women who'd tried to tempt him in really creative ways, but nothing could have prepared him for a woman like Sage.

He was a playboy. That was his role, and he was good at it. Some called him a typical pretty boy, while others called him rugged with a street edge. No matter what labels others gave him or he gave himself, the one consistent factor was that Grayson Ellington was not a pushover and could maintain self-control better than most. Calculated. Precise. Detailed. That was him... except when it came to Sage Langley.

Being alone with Sage undid years of perfecting the type of man he was, each and every time he saw her. She knew him. She knew what buttons to push. She knew what made him happy, what made him sad. There was really nothing he wouldn't trust her with, and that included discussing his insecurities.

What he was learning was that not only did she know all those things about him, but she was also slowly learning what made him aroused. She was perfecting the way she could read him and learning all the seduction tactics that made him weak.

Her hand was resting on his thigh mere inches away from his shaft. God, what he wouldn't give to have her hands cup him. She must have sensed what he was thinking, because she inched her hands even closer. He had his arm around her, and her head was leaning on his chest so he couldn't see her face. She always used to lean on him when they watched movies, but tonight was different. Tonight, he didn't have to worry about the skeptical looks Tate would shoot his way or the intrigued looks from Piper.

Without warning, she slipped her hands in his pants in a movement so quick, he actually didn't see her do it; rather, he felt her hands on him. He inhaled in surprise.

"Sage," he said in a warning tone. At least he hoped it sounded like a warning.

"Shhh." She placed her finger in front of her lips, before placing her hand behind his neck and bringing him in for a kiss. The minute their lips touched, feelings rushed through him that he hadn't felt in eight years.

She rubbed his shaft in up-and-down movements in a tempo similar to the one she was kissing him with. Who was this Sage? Bold. Beautiful. A seductress if he'd ever met one. He wouldn't deny that he'd imagined a moment similar to this many times, but what was happening now was way better than he'd thought it would be.

He whispered her name in between kisses, and her satisfying moans were enough to push him closer to the edge. He needed to regain control of the situation. There was no way he was coming in her hands after years of waiting for an opportunity to be with her.

He broke the kiss to tell her just that but didn't get a chance. Sage took the opportunity to replace her hands with her mouth as her tongue slipped over his tip in the sweetest kiss he'd ever received.

"Oh, shit," he said aloud, unable to hold back those words any longer. Her hands quickly joined her mouth, doubling the torture and causing him to do nothing more than wait for her to finish what she'd started.

"Hmm, you taste just like I imagined," she said between sucks.

"If you keep talking like that, I won't be able to refrain from releasing myself."

She looked into his eyes, her mouth still glued to him. "I'm ready when you are."

He threw his head back, all rationality leaving his body. It only took a few more minutes for him to come in the hardest orgasm he'd ever experienced. Her mouth didn't leave him until she'd lapped up every last drop.

When the quivers began to subside, he finally lifted his head back to look at her and see if he saw any sign of regret. Not only was regret not reflected in her features, her satisfied grin proved she had more she wanted to do.

He wasn't sure how he got the energy, but he swooped her off the couch and carried her into the bedroom. He slowly removed her clothes, taking his sweet time. Undressing Sage was something he'd always known would be an amazing experience. Like opening a well-wrapped Christmas present and realizing it was everything you'd ever wanted.

When she lay in the bed completely naked except for her panties, he stripped himself of his clothes, enjoying the look of appreciation she wore on her face.

He'd always been more of a giver than a taker in the bedroom, so now he wanted her to experience how much he could pleasure her with his mouth. Her panties were the last thing he removed, and when they were gone, he couldn't wait to get his fill of her. He was only centimeters away from her rectangular patch when she put up her hands to stop him.

"Please, Grayson, I'm already wet as hell. I just want you inside me…now."

He gulped. Hard. There was no way he wasn't obliging her wishes.

He protected himself and positioned his body on top of her. "Sage, if I start to hurt you at all, please tell me…" His words trailed off as she grabbed his shaft and put him inside her.

He groaned in satisfaction at the same time that she moaned in pleasure. He couldn't help but look into her eyes as he slowly pulled himself out, just to thrust back inside her. Being inside Sage was indescribable, and he knew without a doubt there would never be another woman who would make him feel so alive.

Chapter 8

Sage almost tossed her magazine across the beach in frustration. Yesterday she'd had an amazing time with Grayson on their trip to Santo Domingo to explore some of the best historical landmarks in the Dominican Republic.

Releasing all those emotions she'd kept bottled up had really put a few things in perspective, and she was so grateful to Grayson for being there for her. She was still a work in progress, but she was feeling freer than she had in years.

"Ugh, this is ridiculous." At one point she'd literally gone years without sex. Even now, she couldn't recall the last time she'd had sex with a man.

Probably because you always compare every man to Grayson. She silenced the voice inside her head, even though she knew it was true. It didn't matter if she dated a Latino, an Italian, a Middle Easterner or an African. Every man she'd met overseas hadn't measured up.

She looked at the sun setting in the distance and moaned again. Grayson had told her he had to take care of some business, since he'd decided to actually meet his client, who really was vacationing in Punta Cana. She'd been lying on the beach for hours under a palm tree waiting for him to get back. It didn't matter that she would probably be avoiding him if he were here. She wanted him to at least be here so that he knew she was avoiding him.

When they had kissed the other day, it had been one of the best kisses she'd ever had in her entire life. Of course, her top three kisses were all kisses from Grayson, but that was beside the point. After making out for about fifteen minutes, Grayson had suggested they retire to their separate rooms. She knew what he was doing. He wanted to make sure that when they made love, it would be because she wanted to and not because she was upset or seeking comfort after talking about her past. Not only was that not the case, but she was pretty sure she was going to pass out from lust if she had to watch him run on the beach again.

She glanced at the house and noticed his car still wasn't there. Since it was getting dark, she had to go inside, but she had news for Grayson Ellington. If he was going to lay on the seduction thick in the beginning and then pull all this platonic let's-not-have-sex-until-we're-ready BS, she was going to have fun without him. And if her plan worked, he wouldn't wait too long to join in.

Grayson glanced at the crowd in the reggae club a few blocks from his vacation home. The club was right outside the gated vacation home area and included vacationers and locals alike.

The Hendersons had kept him way longer than he'd

anticipated, and he had barely been able to concentrate. All the vacation homes had enough distance from each other to maintain privacy, but the area where Sage had been on the beach, so close to the water, could be seen from the top floor of the Hendersons' home, where they kept the office.

There were other people on the beach, but he knew that speck in the distance had been Sage without any further confirmation. During the meeting, he'd imagined himself lying on the beach with her, and after about an hour he was kicking himself for being so stupid and telling her that they had to wait to make love to each other. It had been eight years since he'd last been intimate with her, and here he was, prolonging their wait even more.

He spotted her sitting at the bar swaying to the beat of the music. Even though he was in a hurry to get to her, he stood back and watched her from a short distance. She looked sexy in her pink-and-black dress. She'd pulled her curls all to one side, and even in the dim club lighting she looked breathtaking. A quick glance around the club proved he wasn't the only person to think so.

Suddenly, his favorite Bob Marley song echoed through the speakers. It had been years since he'd been able to enjoy the song at a reggae club instead of on his iTunes playlist. Sage's eyes had landed on his before he even made it across the room to her. She stood from the bar stool, and time seemed to be moving in slow motion as she met him halfway across the dance floor.

Words weren't needed as they began dancing to the beat of the music in a way that proved time didn't mean a thing. Their bodies knew each other and moved in a rhythmic way that had gathered more than a few admirers on the dance floor.

Grayson always loved how passionately Sage danced. She put her entire body into her movements, as did he, which was probably why they'd partnered in dance competitions in the past and succeeded in winning a couple of them. They just worked together.

When Sage turned toward him and placed both arms around his neck, she whispered into his ear, "Bahamas, 2002."

He smiled and placed a soft kiss on her exposed neck before the song picked up in tempo, causing them to dance even harder. Spring break 2002 had been a great trip that he, Tate, Piper and Sage had taken with thirty other college students. Both he and Sage had been in relationships at the time, so they hadn't spoken much while on vacation.

All that changed when they were in a nightclub and the same Bob Marley song played. They'd been on the dance floor with the people they were dating, and by the end of the song, they found themselves on the dance floor alone as others cheered for them to continue dancing.

As the song drew to a close, Grayson wondered if she would end the dance the same way she had back in 2002—with a move that may have seemed like a regular dance move to everyone else, but had turned him on more than any woman ever had before.

On cue, Sage twisted her body, dipped her hips and slowly grinded on his body in a way that made every naughty thought he'd ever had about her come flooding to the forefront of his mind.

"Can we get out of here?" he whispered in her ear. She turned her head toward him and smiled.

"I thought you'd never ask."

Within minutes, they left the dance floor and exited the nightclub.

"I think every person who was watching us dance was waiting to see if we would leave the club."

He raised an eyebrow at Sage as they continued to walk toward his vacation home. "With the way you were dancing, you'd expect anything less?"

She playfully swatted him on the arm. "Um, you can't talk. You were two seconds away from taking off your shirt and throwing it to the ladies in the crowd. I know how you are."

He flashed her his most charming smile. "There's only one lady I want to take off my shirt for."

"Oh, my God, you're ridiculous." She may have been laughing, but he knew his comment had made her feel good.

They weren't even halfway home when it started to rain. Grayson was prepared to remove his shirt to offer her some type of cover, when Sage took off running toward the water.

"What are you doing?"

When she didn't respond, he yelled out to her again as he took off behind her. She had never liked the rain because rain could eventually turn into a thunderstorm. Sage didn't stop until she was close to the water's edge. He wasn't sure what made him slow down when he got near her, but he did, sensing she needed some space.

She outstretched her arms and lifted her head to the sky. "Isn't it amazing?"

He looked up at the sky to try to see what she saw. "Isn't what amazing?"

She dropped her arms to her sides and looked over her shoulder at Grayson. "This moment, here with you. There were times when I was living in other countries, and I'd think of you when it rained and wonder if you were thinking of me, too."

He went to stand next to her, remembering the first time they'd ever kissed in the rain. "I thought about you every time it rained…still do."

"You know what I wonder sometimes?"

"What's that?"

She stepped closer to him. "If all this time, I've been afraid of things that I didn't need to be afraid of."

He shrugged. "I think you're being too hard on yourself. Everyone is afraid of something."

"You've never really seemed to be afraid of anything whatsoever."

"That's not true," he said, looking directly at her. "For years, I was afraid of loving a woman and having her leave me like my mother did."

He watched the emotion drain from her face. "You mean like I did when I left the country."

"Yes and no." He stepped behind her and wrapped his arms around her waist. "No, because I understood why you had to leave and accepted it. Yes, because I was afraid of loving you, but there is nothing about you that reminds me of my mother."

She turned to look up at him. "Thanks for saying that."

Instead of responding, he kissed her softly, and just like all their kisses, it escalated within seconds.

"Come on," he said, leading her to the house. "There's something I want to show you."

When they arrived at the house, Grayson successfully diverted her attention from the fact that there was another car in the driveway and led her through the front door.

"Can you dry off and put on a robe? You can leave on your panties and bra."

She gave him a sly smile. "Oh, you're ready to do something to me now, huh?"

"I'm always ready to do something to you," he said with a laugh. "So go upstairs, and if you want you can even take a quick shower. I only need about twenty minutes."

She nodded in excitement and went up the stairs. Grayson wasted no time opening the front door once he heard the water running upstairs.

"Hello, Mrs. Henderson. She's in the shower, so we only have about twenty minutes to set up."

Licensed massage therapist Paula Henderson smiled. "I only need ten minutes."

After the living room was transformed into an island spa fit for a queen, Grayson escorted Paula to the door.

"I can't thank you enough for helping me with this."

"She's going to love it." Paula returned his hug. "She must be pretty special for you to go through all this trouble. I've never heard you put up much fuss for a woman."

"She's definitely special," he said with a smile. "She's my future wife, but in order to truly win her over I have more work to do."

He glanced at the living room once more, then connected his smart phone to the speakers to play the soothing soundtrack he'd created. Once he was sure everything was exactly how he wanted it, he went to the first-level bathroom to find the bag he'd stashed there before he'd left for the club, and changed into his attire.

Just you wait, Sage Langley, he thought to himself as he started stripping off his clothes. *You're about to see just how romantic I can be.*

Sage exited the bathroom feeling refreshed and curious about what Grayson had in store. She'd heard some banging or movement downstairs when she was in the shower, so she knew he was up to something.

When she reached the bottom stair, she called out for him and received no answer. *Hmm, maybe he wants me to find him.* All the lights in the house were turned off except for a light coming from the living room. As she got closer to the light, she heard music playing softly in the background.

"Grayson, why are all the lights turned off…" Her voice trailed off when she walked into the living room and saw the most appetizing sight she'd ever seen before.

Standing in the middle of the room holding a plate of chocolate-covered strawberries was a shirtless Grayson Ellington wearing a pair of silk boxers.

Oh, lawd. He'd oiled his body, giving him a glow that made her insides twirl in excitement. Each chiseled ab looked so tasty, she wished she could lick every crevice and leave a trail of kisses along the way.

Rose petals were sprinkled on the floor, and a massage table was in the corner of the room, stationed next to a table that seemed to contain a variety of oils. Even though it wasn't usually cold at night, the rain had made it slightly chilly, so it was nice to have the fire going. The entire scene looked so romantic.

The look he had in his eyes was the look he gave her when he wanted her to do something, but in his normal Grayson way, he didn't want to tell her what it was. He wanted her to figure it out. Oftentimes, that quality annoyed her because she would rather he just say what he wanted. Tonight, she didn't mind playing by his rules.

She observed the look on his face once more before stepping closer to him. When she was close enough for him to reach her, he turned around so that his back was to her.

At first, she was a little confused. But then she looked down at the red letters written across his boxers and read the words aloud.

"'Let's be the reason Santa created the naughty list.'"

She giggled at his not-so-subtle way of working Christmas into whatever he had planned. At the sound of her laughter, he turned back to face her, took a strawberry off the plate and placed it close to her mouth. She eagerly took a bite of the sweet dessert, loving the fact that he knew the way to her heart was through her stomach.

"It tastes so good."

His eyes darkened at her comment. "I bet you taste better." He kissed her chocolate-filled mouth. "And tonight, I finally get a chance to see just how delectable you are."

She didn't know why, but she felt so nervous. In the past, she'd seduced him first on more than one occasion. He hadn't been an innocent party, but he hadn't been the Grayson standing before her today.

He placed the strawberries on a nearby table and

picked up a glass of champagne that he handed to Sage. "Tonight, I want to spoil you in a way I should have been doing years ago."

He led her to the massage table and asked her to take off her robe.

I'm so glad I brought some sexy lingerie. She'd chosen to wear her see-through black lace panties and matching bra. When her robe dropped to the floor, Grayson's eyes roamed up and down her entire body, leaving no part untouched.

"You may have to remove this," he said as he slipped his finger underneath her bra strap. She sucked in a deep breath at the close contact. She didn't need to be told twice. Her bra joined her discarded robe.

"Damn, you're beautiful." His appreciation was evident in his eyes. Had she thought about it, she would have thrown on her black stilettos to complete the look.

"Lie facedown on the table so that we can begin." His tone sounded professional, but the looks he was giving her were anything but.

The minute his hands touched her back, she felt her entire body relax. *This is just what I need.* How long had it been since a man had touched her like this? And even then, she was pretty sure she hadn't been touched as intimately as Grayson was touching her now.

His hands felt magical on her body, and he made sure he hit every sweet spot. The playlist of songs he'd chosen were romantic, and each song seemed to represent them in some way.

"You did an amazing job choosing the songs," she said as he asked her to turn over so that he could massage her front side. "Each song is meaningful."

"I was hoping you'd notice." He smiled before he

rubbed the oil in his hands and placed them on her breasts. "I've been listening to this playlist for years."

"Wh-what?" She searched his face. "You didn't just create this?"

He gave her a bashful smile, which almost made her laugh because she was the one exposed on the table with his hands on her breasts. "I originally started the playlist when I was in college."

She squinted in confusion. "So you didn't create this with me in mind?"

"I did," he confirmed, meeting her gaze. "I started the playlist when I was in college, and as my feelings grew, and more songs were released that reminded me of you, I added to the playlist."

In that precious moment, her heart swelled with emotion. The penetrating eyes staring back at her were those of a man who was being open and vulnerable about his feelings. A man who'd waited years to have this moment.

She understood because she felt as if she'd waited her entire life for this moment, as well. The slow, methodical way he was rubbing her breasts combined with the intense way he was looking into her eyes was turning her nerves to a pile of mush.

"It was when I first realized that I was falling for you." He looked at her lips before returning to her eyes. "So even though we were supposed to be nothing more than friends, I couldn't help the way I was feeling about you, and I didn't understand why it was so easy to dismiss other women or forget about them completely...but not you. You stayed in my mind constantly and had a home in the most loving part of my heart. That's where

I kept you." He pointed to his heart. "Right here, until the time was right to tell you how I feel."

"Like now?" she asked as her heart pounded rapidly.

"Like now," he confirmed as he leaned closer to her lips. "Because now I'm sure you know that I've fallen in love with you, and honestly, I should have told you when you told me years ago. Because I was in love with you then and have been for a very, *very* long time."

Chapter 9

He kissed her passionately, but this one felt as if it was filled with so much more emotion than those that had come before. He didn't just feel it in his own actions; he felt it in hers, as well. He wasn't sure the night could get any better until he heard her whisper the words he'd been waiting almost his entire life to hear.

"I'm in love with you, too, Grayson," she said between kisses. "And I have been for a very, *very* long time."

He wanted to finish her massage, but he couldn't wait any longer. He had to taste her. Leaving a trail of wet kisses along her body, he journeyed to the part that needed extra-special attention.

He slid her racy panties down with ease and took a few seconds to just admire the beautiful naked masterpiece of Sage Langley. With an urgency that was becoming all too familiar when he was around Sage, he gently sucked her clit into his mouth. The potent response he received was enough encouragement to make him pull over a nearby chair and drag her legs halfway off the table so that he could cup her butt and really dive in.

"Oh, my God, Grayson, it feels so good."

Good was great, but he wasn't satisfied with just being good. He needed her to feel as if she were the only woman in the world for him because that's exactly what she was.

He dipped his tongue in and out of her sugary center, thinking that she tasted exactly how he thought she would, and he was already addicted.

"I'm close." Her words rushed out in a breathless moan, but he got the message loud and clear. He increased his pressure on her clit, and within moments she was bucking against his mouth and moaning to the ceiling in that voice that made him feel as if everything was going to work out.

He waited until her convulsions subsided before he put two fingers into her center and placed his mouth on her once more.

"Grayson, I don't think I can come again so soon."

Her words died on her lips as his mouth and fingers went to work to stimulate another orgasm. This time, it was his name she was yelling to the ceiling. He gave her a sly grin when she returned back to reality.

"Payback is going to suck for you."

He shook his head in disagreement. "That's where you're wrong." He walked over to where he'd stashed a few condoms and sheathed himself. Then he grabbed the large velour blanket and pillows he'd stashed in the closet and spread them out on the floor. "Our kind of payback is the best type of payback."

He lifted her off the table and gently placed her in the middle of the blanket before positioning himself over her. "Time to make up for lost time." And he definitely meant that in more ways than one.

He entered her in one long, slow thrust. She felt amazing. She felt perfect. She felt like…*home.*

Grayson awoke early the following morning with a huge smile on his face. Last night had gone better than expected, and he was amazed that after over a decade of having strong feelings for each other, in a few days they were able to bring their relationship to another level.

His thoughts were interrupted by a faint ringing noise. It took a few seconds for him to realize it was his cell phone ringing from the second-level bedroom where he'd previously been sleeping.

He left the bed, careful not to awaken Sage. He managed to get to his phone in time only to slightly cringe when he saw it was Tate.

"What's up, man?"

"You say 'what's up' like I haven't been trying to call you for the past few days."

"Well, I wasn't aware I had to check in with you."

"Man, you're testy. Is it that time of the month?"

"Very funny. What do you want?"

"Are you still thinking about stopping over at my mom's for Christmas Eve tonight? I know you said you were flying back in today."

Crap! He'd forgotten all about that. "Listen, Tate, I have to talk to you about something."

"Um, okay."

Grayson took a deep breath. At first, he hadn't understood why Tate even cared if he dated Sage. But then he thought about the hypothetical of Tate wanting to date his younger sister, and then he understood because there was no way in hell he would have let that happen.

"I'm not in Miami."

"Where are you?"

"In Punta Cana. With Sage." The phone grew silent. "Tate, you still there?"

"Yeah, I'm still here, but I'm trying to give you time to explain yourself before I tell you what has to happen next, since I'm sure you aren't in Punta Cana to show Sage the sights."

"You're right, I'm not. I'm here to clear the air about a few things that happened in the past and to let her know how I feel about her."

"What the hell happened in the past?"

"That's not important. What is important is that you know I love Sage with all my heart, and if I think it's something she wants, I plan to marry her one day."

The line grew silent again.

"Tate?"

"Yeah, still here. What did Sage have to say about this?"

"She loves me, too. We actually realize we've loved each other for years, which brings me to the next thing I need to discuss with you."

"Not sure it could get much more intense than what you just said."

"Look, Tate, I promise to love your sister for as long as she will have me, which I hope is for the rest of our lives. You know I gave up my player ways years ago, and quite frankly, there is no other woman in this world for me but her. She sees me for me and accepts all my flaws as a part of me, not something she wants to change. We both grew a lot over the years, but we still have a lot of growing to do. But Sage won't be able to have a future with me if she thinks you're not on board. She values your opinion tremendously, and if she thinks it may jeopardize her relationship with you, she won't give me a second thought."

"So you're asking for my blessing for what, exactly? To date her or to propose?"

"I'm asking for your blessing for both, but first to date so she can get used to the idea of us as a couple."

This time, when the phone grew silent, Grayson didn't say anything.

"Thank God," Tate finally replied. "We definitely have to talk about this more when you get to the States, but I'm glad you finally came to your senses."

"Say what? You knew I loved her?"

"I'm gonna need you to give me more credit than that. I've known how you both felt about each other for years."

"But you told me to stay away from her."

"That's because you were still a player back then. I'll be honest, I think my sister deserves the best, because she is a remarkable woman."

"No argument there."

"But you're also a good man and a good friend who just so happens to love my sister. I called your brother days ago, and I could tell by his confusion that you weren't in Miami, so I figured you'd finally be telling her how you feel."

Grayson ran his long fingers down his face. "This is definitely not how I pictured this conversation going."

"I figured, since you didn't just come right out and tell me. But over the years I've learned that the heart wants what the heart wants, and there is nothing you can do to turn off your feelings. If anything, you can only deter them."

Grayson had a feeling Tate's revelation had something to do with Piper St. Patrick, but he would talk to him about that later.

"One last thing," Grayson said. "Do you think your mom could change her Christmas celebration to tomorrow instead of today?"

"Why?"

"I think I can convince Sage to come tomorrow, but I want to spend some more time with her today so she can prepare herself."

"Oh, okay. That would be great if she agrees. I'll ask Mom, but I'm sure she'll say yes for that reason."

"Great, keep me updated."

He disconnected the call, feeling as though he'd accomplished so much in a short period of time.

"Not exactly the news I wanted to wake up to."

Grayson's face flew to the door to see a thoroughly sexed Sage leaning against the doorjamb.

"How much did you hear?" He patted the bed for her to join him.

"Enough to know that you asked my brother for his blessing for us to date, which means you told him how we feel about each other, and I'm really happy about that. I also heard you say you were going to try to convince me to go home for Christmas."

Judging by the look on her face, she was less than thrilled about that part of things.

* * *

Sage leaned the back of her head against the seat, trying to calm the anxiety she was feeling as they approached Summerland, Michigan.

"I shouldn't have let you talk me into coming here on Christmas Day."

"Everything is going to be fine," Grayson said as he placed a hand over hers. "And I'm very convincing when I want to be."

She couldn't deny that he was right. After he'd told her that going back home for Christmas would help her slay those last demons she had, he'd followed up with a day full of sweet lovemaking. He'd even cooked all her favorite foods and ended the night with a romantic dinner cruise and another full-body massage.

He was doing all he could to prove to her that he loved her and could be the type of man she needed. But he'd always been the perfect man for her, and when he hadn't been showering her with kisses and love, she'd been doing the exact same things for him.

As they drove through the downtown area, Sage had to admit that it hadn't been as bad as she'd thought it would be. Even so, she was still antsy.

"Stop fidgeting. It won't be that bad, I promise."

As they walked to her mother's door, half her nerves were gone. She'd been to her mother's home a thousand times, yet it had been so long since she'd spent Christmas Day with her family. They had barely made it to the door when it swung open and her mom ran out and hugged her.

"Oh, my sweet baby girl, it's so nice to have you here." Her mom pulled Grayson into the hug. "Grayson, I can't thank you enough for finally bringing my baby girl home for Christmas."

Her mom had always loved Grayson as if he were her own son. Sage knew Grayson appreciated his mom's love just as much as she appreciated his dad's. In a way, it brought them even closer than they already were.

"Come on in out of the cold. Everyone is waiting to see you both."

Sage stepped into the house and ran right into a host of aunts, uncles and cousins. *When did everyone start gathering here for Christmas?*

She hugged and kissed relatives she hadn't seen in years. At one point she glanced over at Grayson, who gave her an encouraging smile. She smiled back, but added her own seductive wink that he'd recently told her was one of the sexiest things she did when she thought no one was watching.

"I saw that," said Tate, completely messing up the moment and proving that she wasn't as discreet as she thought.

"Can you try not to bat your eyes at my best friend when I'm around?"

"Oh, okay, I'll do that, big bro. No more winking to show my affection." She walked over to Grayson, who was talking to one of her aunts, and pulled him to her in a quick yet passionate kiss.

"Is that better?" she asked, glancing at Tate.

"Not at all," Tate replied, holding up his hands in defeat. "But I get it. Point taken. Grayson, let's chat for a minute."

As Grayson and Tate went into the office to have what she assumed would be a heart-to-heart about their relationship, Sage sought out her mother. She found her in the kitchen.

"Hey, Mom."

"Hey, sweetie. I'm so glad you're here."

She walked over to her mom and gave her a tight hug. She hugged her mom all the time, but this time, she was hugging her mom on Christmas and building a lasting memory on a day that she'd previously dreaded.

"What was that for?"

"I want to start building good memories around Christmas rather than letting my past memories define my view of what used to be my favorite holiday."

He mom's eyes grew large. "Oh, sweetie, Grayson has really done a number on you in just a few days. If I'd known he could work this fast, I would have suggested you both get together years ago when you first started having these feelings for one another."

Now it was Sage's turn to be surprised. "You knew Grayson and I loved each other?"

Joanne Langley gave her daughter a look of disbelief before she resumed peeling potatoes. "You see, that's the main thing that's wrong with your generation. You think you were the first to do everything. Just because I'm old doesn't mean I don't know true love when I see it. Although at first, what I saw in your eyes and Grayson's was pure lust, so I'm glad it turned to love and wasn't only about sex."

"Okay, this conversation officially got awkward."

"Oh, honey, don't be so naive. We can talk about sex. Speaking of which, when will I get my grandbabies?"

"Mom, it's not like we're engaged right now. Besides, Tate is the oldest. Get on him."

"Child, please, your brother is waiting for Piper to

divorce her husband, and until she does, he isn't going to truly commit to another woman."

Sage gave her mom a blank stare. "You know what? We need to chat so you can catch me up on everything I missed now that I'm back in Michigan."

"Oh, I can update you on a few things now…"

"Sorry to interrupt." Grayson entered the kitchen, and Sage's mouth watered at the way he looked in the black sweater and jeans he was wearing. That man could sport a trash can, and she'd still want to lick every nook and cranny of his body. "Can I borrow Sage?"

"I was actually just leaving," her mom said as she kissed her on the cheek before exiting the kitchen.

Grayson placed a soft kiss on her lips. "I have a gift for you, but I have to put out a disclaimer."

"What's that?"

"Do you remember when you and Piper visited me and Tate in college, and you and I stayed up all night talking after Piper and Tate had gone to sleep?"

"Of course I remember that night. We even took a walk around campus."

"We did." He pulled an envelope out of his pocket. "Open this."

She shot him a skeptical look before she opened the envelope. When she did, she couldn't help the laugh that escaped her lips. She read the note aloud.

"'Will you officially go out with me so that one day *very* soon, I can make you my wife? Please circle yes or no.'"

"Okay, and now open your gift." This time he pulled a large jewelry box from the back of his jeans pocket. She wasted no time opening the box.

"Oh, my goodness," she said as she picked up the diamond necklace and bracelet. "This is beautiful."

He helped her put them both on. "Do you understand your gift?"

She looked from the bracelet on her hand to the letter, then to Grayson. *What in the world does our talk that night have to do with these gifts?* Suddenly, it dawned on her.

"Oh, Grayson, I think I get it." She picked up the letter and a pen from the counter and circled "yes." "That night, I told you that a boy had never given me one of the notes in school that said 'please circle yes if you like me and no if you don't,' and I always felt like I missed out because Piper had gotten them in school."

"Yes, that's exactly what you told me."

"I also told you that when a man proposed to me, my diamond ring better not be the first diamond he buys me." She studied his eyes in disbelief. "I was just talking that night. I wasn't really trying to drop hints."

"I know," Grayson said, bringing her in for a hug. "But I wanted you to understand that I will always listen to everything you tell me. I made a mental note that day, and I was hoping that this moment would come so that I could make those wishes come true."

As she gazed into the eyes of the man she loved, there was no doubt in her mind that she was staring into the eyes of her future husband. She pulled him in for a kiss, and as she did so, she thought about the fact that Grayson had made this the best Christmas she'd ever had.

* * * * *

REQUEST YOUR FREE BOOKS!

2 FREE NOVELS
PLUS 2 *FREE GIFTS!*

KIMANI ™
ROMANCE

Love's ultimate destination!

KROM15

Bailey wondered what there was about Walker that was different from any other man. All it took was the feel of his hand on her shoulder... His touch affected her in a way no man's touch had ever affected her before. How did he have the ability to breach her inner being and remind her that she was a woman?

Personal relationships weren't her forte. Most of the guys in these parts were too afraid of her brothers and cousins to even think of crossing the line, so she'd only had one lover in her lifetime. And for her it had been one and done, and executed more out of curiosity than anything else. She certainly hadn't been driven by any type of sexual desire like she felt for Walker.

There was this spike of heat that always rolled in her stomach whenever she was around him, not to mention a warmth that would settle in the area between her legs.

Even now, just being in the same vehicle with him was making her breasts tingle. Was she imagining things or had his face inched a little closer to hers?

Suggesting they go for a late-night ride might not have been a good idea, after all. "I'm not perfect," she finally said softly.

"No one is perfect," he responded huskily.

Bailey drew in a sharp breath when he reached up and rubbed a finger across her cheek. She fought back the slow moan that threatened to slip past her lips. His hand on her shoulder had caused internal havoc, and now his fingers on her face were stirring something to life inside her that she'd never felt before.

She needed to bring an end to this madness. The last thing she wanted was for him to get the wrong idea about the reason she'd brought him here. "I didn't bring you out here for this, Walker," she said. "I don't want you getting the wrong idea."

"Okay, what's the right idea?" he asked, leaning in even closer. "Why did you bring me out here?"

Nervously, she licked her lips. He was still rubbing a finger across her cheek. "To apologize."

He lowered his head and took possession of her mouth.

Don't miss
BREAKING BAILEY'S RULES
by New York Times *bestselling author*
Brenda Jackson, available November 2015 wherever
Harlequin® Desire books and ebooks are sold.

www.Harlequin.com